The Tragedy of Macbeth

A novel based on the work of William Shakespeare

R.A. Wilson

Shouldn't You Be Reading?

AlyMur Productions ™

Published by AlyMur Productions™
AlyMur.com

Copyright 2013 by R.A. Wilson
Discover other titles by R.A. Wilson at RavinSaga.com

ISBN-10: 0692451374
ISBN-13: 978-0692451373
ASIN: B0091YU9PW

Books by R.A. Wilson

Ravin Saga

The World of Ildor
Endospore

The Fury of Pride
Unbreakable Pride
Joyless Pride (Coming 2015)
Bent Pride (Coming 2015)
Broken Pride (Coming 2016)
Pride's Wrath (Coming 2016)

Shakespeare Novelizations

The Tragedy of Macbeth

Other

Wal-Mart Book of Ethics Abridged Edition

To my Grandma Mary for reminding me after all of these years how long it takes to write a book.

Table of Contents

Book 1

Chapter 1

Though dawn cracks the night, the sun's warming rays cannot reach the cold shadow upon the ground. Occasional flashes of lightening reveal a frozen moment burned fleetingly into one's eyes, dragging on blindness in the intervening time. Looking up during these moments of sight show thick clouds like dark smoke billowing to overcast the land. They carry the promise of a deluge that will soak anyone and everything caught outside when the heavens begin to cry. A precursor to the terrible downpour only moments away, the storm flashes brightly once again.

The booming thunder that follows shakes the ground, heralding in the rain, which begins to fall in a drumming of large, cold, raindrops. The darkness deepens even more, swallowing all but the flashes of light the storm itself brings. The hilltop beneath the sky is illuminated in another blinding flash. It has been made barren under the marching feet of an army that passed by merely the day before. And now the rain quickly turns the hill's exposed dirt into viscous mud.

On the hilltop, three old hags approach one another, seemingly not harried by the storm but instead reveling in it. Each are dressed alike, wearing clothes that have long since decayed into old and moldy rags that hang from their thin and seemingly weak frames. The rags have been added on to cover the previous soiled cloth, leaving the old women to appear bulky in the layers. Their faces are old and dark, their thin hair hoary, and their shoulders slumped from long lives spent on hard paths. Their aged faces are covered by thin, wispy beards of hair that would look at home on a long dead corpse.

The first raises her arms up in greeting and speaks in a creaking voice. "Well met, under the thunder on the hilltop."

The second and third grin in reply, showing rotten and missing teeth.

The second says, "It shall be as we foresaw at our last meeting. The events have come to pass."

The third adds, "Then we shall need to meet once more to speak the prophesy to Macbeth. He is the one who must listen."

"When shall that be? Under the thunder, the lightening, or shall it be in the rain?" the first asks.

The second answers, "After the battle the army marches to, when the victor emerges. We shall meet then."

The third looks across the horizon, her eyes growing unfocused, seeing that which is hidden in the dark. "That will come before the sun sets on this day. They lock in battle as we speak."

The second declares, "Then let the meeting be on the field, among the corpses, two days after the battle. It is a fitting setting for such deeds as any would be."

The third cackles in joy. "And it will be there that Macbeth comes to us."

The first hag looks behind her, into the darkness, her attention drawn by some sound only she can hear. The second and third also are distracted away momentarily before the three return their attentions to one another.

The shadowy outline of a cat emerges from the rain. Darker than even the night sky, the cat's form is visible only as a shadow in the downpour. It comes from behind the first hag and sits, licking its front paw as it waits, unconcerned with the falling rain. A toad emerges from behind the second witch, looking much larger than a toad should naturally grow. Nothing comes from behind the third, but still she hears her familiar's call.

3

"I am coming, Graymalkin," the first says to the cat, waving a hand dismissively.

"Paddock also calls," the second says to the first.

The third exclaims, calling to her familiar, who has yet to arrive, "I am here!"

Pulling their attention back to one another, the witches say in unison, "That which is fair is now foul, and that which is foul is now fair. Fly! Take to the fog and filthy air. After the battle we shall meet Macbeth to bear witness and ensnare."

The three fade from sight as if by some otherworldly sorcery, and their familiars vanish with them.

Chapter 2

The sword's tip bites deeply, piercing the weak point between plates of armor under the armpit. Blood flows down the blade from the wound. Through the soldier's visor, Malcolm, the king's son, sees the other's eyes grow wide in both surprise and understanding. Fear overtakes his mind. The man falls to his knees as the blade is withdrawn, and Malcolm moves on to his next opponent. The soldier even crumples to the ground with no hope of stanching the blood flowing under the armor, and the world turns black for him seconds later.

Malcolm steps into another guard position, blocking a downward swung blade with his own, crossing it above his head. Malcolm swings his blade to the left, forcing the soldier's sword with it. He then kicks with his right leg, landing it just above the foot on the other man, making him stumble back and almost fall. Malcolm presses forward and rams with his shoulder into the other's chest, tumbling him over.

Before Malcolm can finish his opponent, another soldier shoves into him. He takes a couple short, choppy steps to the side to keep his feet under him and turns back to his assailant. A sword is lunging toward his midsection. Malcolm, with the thoughtless action only brought by unending training, swipes his own blade down to push the attack aside while he pulls his chest back and turns sideways. The weapon stabs into thin air.

Malcolm attacks, striking his own weapon into the other's groin, cutting through the thin armor at the joint. The other falls to

5

the ground. Malcolm swings back to his first opponent, who now attempts to stand in the cumbersome armor. The king's son stabs down with his blade, and it slides between the breastplate and helmet, plunging deeply into the man's torso. His body immediately goes limp and falls.

Pulling his sword out, the prince swings it around with all the force he can muster and cracks it into the helm of the second man, sending him all the way to the ground. Not sure if he is dead or merely knock out, Malcolm finishes his grisly business with a quick strike to the back of the neck, making sure he will not rise again.

Looking for his next victim, Malcolm sees the battle raging all around him. He continues dancing amid the soldiers, his blade flashing from one opponent to the next. His honor guard watches his flank as he pushes deeper into the enemy numbers. Each guardsman is a veritable powerhouse with a blade, even more skilled than Malcolm, as they all train together to fight as a unit.

Malcolm pulls his blade out of the visor of his last challenger as an axe hits his back plate, denting the mudded and blooded steel. He falls to the ground and immediately curls up to keep his body protected. His guardsmen rush in to all sides quickly, some holding back the attackers while two others pull him back to his feet. Standing again, the king's son sees the axe wielder already dispatched, headless.

Malcolm pushes forward, back into the line, blocking a strike aimed at one of his guardsmen. Malcolm steps in close, both of their swords rendered useless at this range, and pulls a dagger from his belt. The blade rips forth into the underside of the man's chin, piercing all the way to the hilt. Malcolm's wide eyes scan for his next challenger.

Someone bumps him from behind, making him stumble forward and almost impaled upon a sword of an otherwise distracted enemy. Malcolm ends the man's life before turning to see what hit him and finds the remainder of his guardsmen fallen to the ground. Even his banner carrier lays in the blood and mud, half of his skull gone. In merely seconds, he is alone in a sea of enemies.

6

Only now does he realize how far ahead of the column he had pushed in his battle lust.

The fear felt from before the battle comes back now, but he does not yield. Malcolm fights harder, for now he fights only for his life. A sword finds purchase between the armor plats upon his shoulder from behind. His sword arm goes numb, and the blade falls from his grasp. A ring of enemy soldiers surround him, but they do not move to finish the prince.

Malcolm knows they will not kill him now. They realized who he is, but that is reason for concern in itself. He will not be killed, but he will be captured, and that sometimes can be the worst of options.

The line of his would-be captors falls apart as a sword wielding countryman of Malcolm's breaks through, slaying two enemy soldiers before they even knew he was there. Malcolm reaches down and picks up his own blade again with his off arm.

"My lord!" the soldier yells, and Malcolm sees by his armor the man is a captain of the army.

"Captain, to me!" Malcolm orders while raising his blade in a defensive posture.

The captain moves beside the prince, protecting his flank as they slowly retreat. More countrymen break through the line behind them and surround the king's son, soldiers ordered forward by the captain who had outdistanced them in the effort to save the prince.

The battle disappears to Malcolm behind a wall of steal and flesh. He quickly is in the safety of his own army as it surges forward, their castle's wall merely a hundred feet away before they stop their fleeing. The captain comes beside him once again. "My lord, we need to get you to the surgeons. That wound looks ghastly."

"I'm fine, captain."

"I don't think so, my lord."

"I could order you to belay that."

"And I could say I didn't hear you over the battle." The captain calls to his men, "Escort him to the surgeons in the castle.

Do not let anyone come near the prince until then."

The soldiers salute and march off with the prince, leaving the captain. As soon as the prince is lost from sight, the captain places a hand on his own midsection, where a poleaxe had pierced his armor and a trickle of blood flows. He had kept it hidden from the prince. The captain would not be ordered to the surgeons himself. He would not retreat from the battle, not when it nearly is a complete route of the enemy. His duty to king and country over his own life.

The army about the captain erupts in cheering. The captain looks up to the walls and sees the good thane Macbeth on the walls, carrying something in both hands before him like a trophy.

****

Macbeth smiles down upon the army he captains. In his hands is the head of a man, the man that caused this battle to be necessary in which so many countrymen died. The enemy itself used to be countrymen, but no longer. Macbeth cannot think of them as such after following the traitorous Macdonwald in his coup d'état against the crown.

The thane raises above his own helm the head of Macdonwald, and the cheering from the men below intensifies. Satisfied in their reverie, Macbeth pounds the head down upon one of the spikes on the castle wall, piercing it all the way to the top inside the skull. He pulls his sword from its scabbard, thrusts it into the sky, and shouts, "For Duncan!"

The army below begins to chant the name of their king as Macbeth continues to pump his blade into the dark sky. Macbeth looks over the field, witnessing the last remains of the fighting. His partner on the field, Banquo, still leads his men against the last few remaining soldiers that stand against them, but the day is taken. The insurrection is done with the death of Macdonwald.

A horn blast draws his attention just then. In the distance, Macbeth sees another army just rising over the next hill. In the heat of battle, nobody noticed the approach of another enemy. Macbeth cannot believe his eyes, seeing the banners of the Norwegians flying in the wind. At first he thinks he is having one of his fits, the hallucinations he has when under stress, but others begin to cry out at seeing the other army.

He smiles despite himself. The day is not yet done, and he is ready for more. His men rally on the ground before the castle, and Macbeth hurries down to join then, to lead them forward once again into the fray of battle for king and country.

****

A large pavilion colored red stands in the middle of the army's encampment, host to King Duncan and his sons, Malcolm and Donalbain. The nobleman Lennox is there with them in attendance. The king is an aging man, with long hair coming from under his crown, and a simple goatee on his chin. His clothes are rich, full of reds and blues, and many encrusted gems are on his personage in jewelry and pins.

Donalbain wears extravagant pieces of armor that are more for looks than actual use with gold leafing and lettering. He does not carry a sword, and over his shoulders rests a cape of royal blue.

Malcolm is another matter. He wears a mere tunic and pants, loose fitting as to not put pressure on his wounds. There is a bandage wrapped around his forehead, and his left arm is in a sling from injuries he suffered three days prior at the battle. He was taken to the surgeons as ordered and treated for a day and a half before being returned to his father, the king.

King Duncan sits on a wooden throne, his sons standing off to either side behind him, enthralled by every word spoken from the Thane of Ross as he recalls the battle to the king. The Thane of Angus stands beside Ross, remaining quiet as his peer speaks. The only other people in the pavilion are the attendants to the royalty, who hustle about taking care of the crown's needs and whims. Lennox also stands near by listening.

"But Macbeth showed no fear as he met the Norwegian attack shot for shot. It was as if he was the goddess of war's husband, untiring and unrelenting. He finally broke the enemy's spirits and split their lines, sending them running."

Duncan exclaims, "Great tidings indeed!"

Ross continues, "And now Sweno, the Norwegian king, wants a treaty with us. He begs for our pardon."

"Then I shall send my response in all good time. Letting him wait and sweating a little will do him some good," Duncan responds, pleased. He peaks his hands in front of his face as a large smile cracks his visage.

"Beg your pardon, sire, but he was already treated with," Ross says, bowing his head.

"Indeed?" Duncan strokes his trimmed beard. "I do not recall my royal personage answering King Sweno. And who is king with the authority to treat as such? Isn't it I?"

"Yes, sir, it is you, and no I don't recall your words being sent. Your field commanders took it upon themselves to answer on your behalf." Ross falls silent, waiting, he hopes, for the king's accent.

The king stares hard, anger radiating from his every pore. Duncan lowers his arms and sits back, looking down his nose at Ross. "And exactly what reply was given?"

Ross releases a breath he did not realize he had been holding. "He was informed that we wouldn't even let him bury his dead until he retreats back to Saint Colme's Inch."

The king jumps up, standing before the throne. "My commanders not only overstep themselves, but they are that lenient?" Duncan shouts. "Perhaps we allow any usurper and betrayer to confront us with no repercussions then. Where would that leave the realm?"

In a shaking voice, Ross adds, "He was also told he must pay the royal treasury back the cost of the campaign, totaling a thousand pounds."

Duncan stares at Ross in silence for a few seconds before roaring in laughter. "Now that sounds like my men! I suppose all will be forgiven then." The king sits back down.

Ross asks, "And what would you have us do with the Thane

10

of Cawdor? He is in custody, but he betrayed us to Sweno, sire. He helped the Norwegians build in force upon our lands. He may even have enticed Macdonwald to rebel in the first place."

"The Thane of Cawdor will never again be able to betray me. He is to be executed, and I hope he dies as the Thane he was, not the traitorous swine he became."

"I will see to it, my lord," Ross replies.

"And all of his titles and lands will be given to our victor on this day. Tell Macbeth that Cawdor is now his."

Ross bows deeply. "You are most generous, your highness. I will not tarry any longer. It is a day's ride to the army." Ross leaves the pavilion with Angus right behind.

Duncan laughs in delight. "Did you hear that, my sons? It is over. Breathe in relief that the realm will be made whole again."

Chapter 3

The sun rises over another day to once again remain hidden by thick storm clouds. The rain does not fall now, but the thunder still booms. Each flash of lightening brightens the dead and nearly dead lying over the field. The bodies are clad in two different types of armor, where the majority of it is from Scotland, and a tithe of them is Norwegian.

Gleefully dancing among the corpses, their feet squishing in equal parts rain and blood on the muddy ground, are the three hags.

The first witch asks, "I didn't think to ask the other day, but I just must know. Where have you been traveling, dear sister?"

The second answers in delight, clasping her hands together as an overexcited school girl. "Killing pigs. I love how they squeal."

The third asks the first, "And what of you?"

"I was at the coast, in a drab city. No garbage or homeless on the streets at all to play with."

"Sounds ghastly," the second says in horror.

"It was. I did not have much time to wallow there however. Before I had to come meet with you, my sisters, I met the wife of a sailor. He was gone, sailed away as the master of a ship named *Tiger*."

"Did you steal her eyes?" the third asks.

"Nay, but I wish I had. You see, she was eating chestnuts. She just sat there, munching on them. I told her to give me them, but the fat whore told me to get away, as if I was something to loathe. She didn't even have any dirt in her hair or on her face."

"Ugh!" exclaims the third.

"How disgusting," the second replies.

"Surely you did not allow that filthy fat thing to get away with such disrespect," the third says.

"Perhaps you boiled her up?" the second suggests.

"Nay, sisters. But listen to this. Her husband sailed off to Aleppo. I will chase him down in a kitchen strainer as my vessel in the guise of a tailless rat and do things to him when I catch up!"

The second says with great pride, "I'll give you some wind to help catch him."

"How nice of you."

The third, to not be outdone, replies, "And I will give you even more wind."

The first rolls her eyes and clicks her tongue. "I already control all of the other winds, and every port they blow from in every direction a sailor can head. I'll catch him and drain out his life. He won't be able to sleep either day or night. He will live as a cursed man for eighty-one weeks, wasting away in agony."

The second says, "The sweetness of that sorrow."

Smiling, the first says, "Although I can't make his ship disappear, I can still make his journey miserable. Oh!" she exclaims as she digs in her rags. "Looky here what I have!"

"Show me, show me!" the second squeals.

The first opens her hands, and something fleshy and round rolls from her palm onto her fingers. "It is the thumb of a sailor who was drowned while trying to return home."

The third smiles. "His thumb! What a wonderful prize." Her head snaps to the side, looking off into the distance. "Ah! It is time. Macbeth comes!"

The three dance in a circle around each other, chanting, "We weird sisters, hand in hand, travelers of the sea and land, thus dance around and around. Three times to you, and three times to me, and then three again, to make nine." They stop dancing but remain in a circle. "The charm is ready."

Macbeth comes down the hill, talking with his fellow captain Banquo, having not yet seen the witches. Macbeth's voice carries over the stillness of the dead to the witches' ears. "I have never seen a day that was so glorious and foul all at the same time. We were victorious against the traitors, but the cost. So many dead. Why do we have to fight against our own?"

Banquo, lost in his own thoughts, asks, "Just how far have we walked from the castle anyway? I expected us back by now."

Macbeth sees the witches and stops, placing his hand across Banquo's chest to stop his friend as well. Banquo looks up to see what spooked Macbeth. He says aside to his friend, "What manner of creatures are these? They're so withered. And their clothes look like they crawled out of a bog."

"I'm not sure," Macbeth answers.

"They don't look like they are part of this world, but here they stand. What are they?" Banquo shouts out to the hags, "Are you alive? Can you speak?"

The witches smile but do not offer a reply short of placing fingers to their lips in a sign to remain silent.

Banquo shouts again. "Are you human? You look like women, but you have beards. What are you?"

Macbeth says, "Spirit or human, if you can, speak to me. What kind of creatures are you?"

The first witch lowers her hand and speaks. "All hail, Macbeth! Hail to you, Thane of Glamis."

Macbeth recoils as these creatures know his name. Before he can react further, the second calls out as well.

"All hail, Macbeth! Hail to you, Thane of Cawdor."

Macbeth glances at Banquo, confusion covering his face. "What are they...."

He is cut off as the third rattles, "All hail, Macbeth! Future king."

Macbeth's head snaps back to the witches. "King? Did she just say king?"

14

Banquo smirks. "My dear Macbeth, why are you so startled by the nice things they are saying?" He calls out to the witches, "Are you merely illusions, or are you flesh and blood? I need to know. Is this glorious future true you promise to my friend?"

"Banquo, I don't think we should…," Macbeth tries.

"Silence, my friend. Don't be so selfish." He calls out again. "Dear creatures, what about me? If you know what shall come, then tell my future."

The witchs together cry out, "Hail!"

Banquo smiles in glee.

The first says, "You are lesser than Macbeth, but at the same time greater."

The second says, "You are not as happy as Macbeth, but at the same time happier."

The smile vanishes. "What is this nonsense," Banquo replies in growing agitation, "You tell him he shall be king, but I'm just happier and greater while being lesser. Nonsense."

The third proclaims, "Your descendants will be kings, though you shall not. So all hail Macbeth and Banquo!"

The first shouts, "Banquo and Macbeth, all hail!"

"What does that mean?" Banquo yells. "I demand answers!"

As a dream that overstayed its welcome into the daylight, the three begin to fade, becoming insubstantial.

"Wait!" Macbeth yells, finding his voice once more. "I have so many questions. Tell me more! I am the Thane of Glamis. But you call me the Thane of Cawdor as well. He is alive, and a rich and powerful man. And being king is impossible. Where did you learn these strange things?" His voice grows higher as he continues in greater resignation. "And why do you stop us in this desolate place with your prophetic greetings? Answer me. I command you!"

But the witches finish fading into the void.

Banquo asks, "Where did they go?"

Macbeth looks into the sky. "Into thin air, my friend. Melted away like a breath in the wind." He closes his eyes tight. "How I wish they stayed."

"Were those creatures really just here? I doubt my own eyes and ears." He looks to Macbeth. "Are we both on drugs?"

"Your children will be kings."

"Yes, and they said you will be king. I don't think we need to place much hope in our hallucination," Banquo says.

"Were they a hallucination? That is something I know about, but these three appeared to be something different." Macbeth asks, "And I am the Thane of Cawdor as well. Isn't that what they said? I doubt everything I think I heard."

"That is exactly what I heard. Could we really have dreamed them together?"

"I do not know," Macbeth says. "Let's return to the castle and discus this further."

****

A voice calls out to them as they enter the court yard of the castle. "Gentlemen!"

Banquo and Macbeth see thanes Ross and Angus approach through the crowds of people shuffling around completing tasks. The four men greet each other warmly.

Ross says, "The king was happy to hear of your success, Macbeth. Your exploits against the rebels has left him speechless! To think, you stood against the rebels, and then the army of Norway and showed not the least bit of fear as you chopped your opponents down. Messenger after messenger delivered news of your bravery to the king."

Angus says, "The king has sent us to collect you. You are to be thanked and presented to the king for your reward."

Ross beams. "As for a taste of what is to come, I've been asked to call you the Thane of Cawdor. So hail the Thane of Cawdor! The title is now yours."

Banquo looks at his friend, eyes wide in wonder. He whispers, "Can the devil tell the truth?"

16

Macbeth shrugs off his friend and says to Angus and Ross, "The Thane of Cawdor is still alive. Surely you are mistaken. Why are you calling me by his title?"

Angus replies, "The man who was the Thane of Cawdor is alive still, but not much longer. He has been sentenced to death, and the traitor deserves to die. I don't know if he fought with the Norwegians, or if he aided the rebels, but he admitted his treason. He's finished. So congratulations, Thane of Cawdor."

Macbeth says to himself in shock, "It's just like they said."

"It is." Banquo agrees aside to him.

"I'm the Thane of Glamis, and now the Thane of Cawdor. And the best part has yet to come!" Macbeth does not even try to hide his excitement as he turns back to Angus and Ross. "Thank you for the news, gentlemen."

Banquo grabs his shoulder and whispers into his ear. "I'm not so certain about this."

Macbeth turns back to him. "Aren't you beginning to hope that your children will be kings? The witches promised I would be Thane of Cawdor, and so I am."

"If you trust what they say, you may be on your way to being king yourself, but this whole thing is strange. Well, despite the obvious, their otherworldliness and vanishing and such. They are agents of evil. They are telling us truths to lead us into destructions. What else can this all be?"

"Banquo...."

"No. I need to think on this." He looks back to Ross and Angus, who gaze upon them awkwardly for their whisperings. By way of explanation, Banquo says, "Look at my friend. He is in a daze. Macbeth is not used to his new titles. He has been the Thane of Glamis for only a short while, and to have this given to him as well! To him, his titles are like new clothes that have to be broken in."

Ross says, "Such a philosopher warrior."

Banquo replies, "I'm ready to travel to the king whenever you are, Macbeth."

The new Thane of Cawdor looks up to the others. "I beg your pardon. I was distracted. Kind gentlemen, I won't forget your pains of bringing me this kindly news. I will be ready shortly. I have a little business I must take care of first. I'll be ready half past the hour." He pulls Banquo to the side and says, "Think about what happened today, and when you have had time to consider it all, we need to talk."

"Absolutely."

"Until then, we have said enough."

Macbeth walks away from the others, lost in thought. Could he become king? The witches proclaimed his ascension to Thane of Cawdor, and Macbeth can see no evil in this. It is a great thing that which has happened. But how could he become king? Duncan is alive and well, as are his heirs. It would take murder to change that, and at the thought, Macbeth's hair stands on end, and his heart pounds in his chest. He finds himself growing frightened of the thoughts running through his mind.

Quietly, Macbeth proclaims to himself, "If fate wants me to be king, perhaps fate will just make it happen and I won't have to do anything. One way or another, what's going to happen is going to happen." He calls out, "Send Seyton to me. I have a task for him."

He retreats to his temporary office in the castle to draft a letter to his wife, the Lady Macbeth.

18

Chapter 4

Malcolm returns to the pavilion and bows to his father. His brother rises from his reclined position to listen as well.

King Duncan asks, "Has the former Thane of Cawdor been executed yet? Have the people in charge of that come back?"

"My king, the deed has been done. I did not speak to those executing him but did speak with someone who saw Cawdor's beheading. The Thane confessed his treason openly and begged your highness's forgiveness and repented."

Duncan lifts his chin. "As he should have. Did he at least die well?"

"He never did anything in his whole life as well as he died. He looked like someone who was tossing away his most cherished possession as if it were nothing but garbage. It was a fitting end for a man of such stature."

Duncan nods in acceptance. "There's no way to really know another man's mind. I trusted Cawdor completely. At least in death he was the man I thought. And what of Captains Macbeth and Banquo?"

In answer, Malcolm waves forward a herald from behind the tent flap. The herald calls out, "Your highness. I present Captain Macbeth, Thane of Glamis, Thane of Cawdor. Captain Banquo. Thane Ross. Thane Angus."

"Excellent. Let them enter."

The herald steps aside as the four men enter. Malcolm greets them personally before stepping aside, leaving them before the king.

Duncan smiles warmly and greets them. "My most worthy kinsman, Macbeth. I feel guilty."

"My lord?"

"I was just thinking how you have done so much for me in such a short time that I haven't been able to properly reward you. In fact, my payment to you so far would only be enough if you have done a tithe of what you have for the crown."

"You do me too much honor, your majesty." Macbeth bows low.

"No. I don't. I owe you more than I can ever repay."

"Having the opportunity to serve you is its own reward. It is your duty to accept what we owe you. You are like our father, and as your children, we owe you. Doing everything to protect you is merely what we should."

"Good man. You are most welcome here, and I shall grant you favor. I have planted the seeds of great fortune in you, Macbeth, by naming you Thane of Cawdor, and I will make sure you grow." King Duncan shifts his attention to Banquo. "Noble sir, I have not forgotten of you, a man who deserves no less than Macbeth, and everyone should know it. Let me gift you with my love and good will."

"Then anything great I accomplish will be credited to you, your majesty." Banquo bows deeply.

"I feel tearful with joy," the king says. "In this ostentatious moment, I want my sons, kinsmen, thanes, and all others close to me to witness this. I bestow my kingdom onto my eldest son, Malcolm. Today, I name him the prince of Cumberland. But it is not just Malcolm we honor today. Titles of nobility will be granted to all who deserve them."

"Hazzah!" they all yell in celebration.

The king turns to Macbeth and addresses him. "Let's go to your castle at Inverness, my dear thane, where I shall become even more obliged to you for your hospitality."

20

"My king." Macbeth nods his head in servitude. "I shall not be joyous unless I am at your service. I will go ahead and bring my good wife the news of your coming. I shall be off to prepare."

"My worthy Cawdor!" King Duncan beams.

Macbeth turns and leaves the pavilion, thinking furiously of the king's decisions. Malcolm, the prince of Cumberland! Only stepping over the prince would grant Macbeth the kingdom, or he will have to give up such thoughts as the prince stands in his path. The desire boils in his mind, and he hopes to all creation that such desire is hidden deep inside to not be discovered. More than anything else, he hopes to not realize what he knows he will do, that horrible thing Fate has called for him.

Before leaving, Macbeth sends a messenger ahead to tell the Lady Macbeth of the king's pending arrival.

Back inside the pavilion, the king says to Banquo, "You are right. Macbeth is every bit as valiant as you claim. His commendations match his deeds finally, as hard as that is to accomplish. He is a man without equal."

"Yes," Banquo says. "It is as your majesty says. I am afraid he is a man who will accomplish much."

Chapter 5

Inside the castle at Inverness, Lady Macbeth paces in her room, reading a letter sent by her husband for the third time since receiving it the day before. "And so I have learned the witches' prophetic words are true. Messengers from the king arrived and greeted me as the Thane of Cawdor! That is exactly how the witches had greeted me before calling me the future king. I thought to share this news with you, my dearest partner in greatness, so you can rejoice with me in the immensity that is promised us. Keep this secret between us and farewell."

She lowers the letter. "My dear Macbeth. So you are the Thane of Glamis and now Cawdor. Wondrous news! And you shall be king as promised. I only fear that you may have too much kindness to seize the crown. You must strike aggressively at the first opportunity or your ambition will fail."

She walks to the window and looks out into the courtyard. "You want to be powerful, but I fear you do not have the malice these events would call for. You want to be powerful but only as a good man. You don't want to cheat, but you desire what is not yours to have. My Macbeth, you will be too afraid to do what needs to be done. Otherwise, your goals will merely remain ambition and not reality." She steps away from the windowsill.

"I know my husband well. You would want it done for you, to let fate work it out. But things do not happen that way. Hurry home to me, so I can persuade you, to talk you out of the misgivings I know are holding you back from taking the crown. It's what we must do. Fate and witchcraft both demand you to be king. Who are we to deny it?"

A rapping on the door precedes it opening to admit a servant girl. "Beg your pardon, my lady. I bring news from your lord husband."

"Out with it then."

"The king will be here tonight."

"What?" True shock registers on her face. "You must be mad to say such things! Macbeth is with the king, so he would have told me they were coming. Would he not?"

"I'm sorry, my lady, but our thane and king are coming to us now. He sent a messenger ahead that hurried himself out of breath. He could barely impart the message for you, my lady."

"Then take good care of the messenger! He brings great news." A shadow falls over her face, "Unlike the one in the cellar."

The servant bows and departs, leaving Lady Macbeth alone once more.

"Glory to my lord husband and I! The king comes on the heels of the prophecy. But my husband will need prompting. Come to me spirits that tend to murderous thoughts and make me less of a woman and more of a man. Fill me with dire spitefulness. Thicken my blood and stop it in my veins to cease the beating of my human heart and its flow of remorse. Make it so no human compassion can stop me from accomplishing what my husband will achieve. Murderous demons, from wherever you hide, waiting to do evil things, turn my breast milk to a vile poison. Caress the night with the darkest smoke of hell, so my knife will not see the wound it cuts, and the heavens cannot see and cry out to stay my hand."

She leaves her rooms and calls the castle's staff to action.

******

When Macbeth returns home, his wife greets him in the study. "Great Thane of Glamis! Worthy Thane of Cawdor! I can barely believe the good fortune that has fallen to us."

"I can barely believe it myself! The great luck." Macbeth rejoices with her.

They embrace each other, and Lady Macbeth whispers into his ear, "And you shall be king!"

He steps back, appearing a little shaken. "So my letter has reached you then?"

"Seyton placed it in my hand himself, and it sped me away from the present, to a future where it already has happened."

"Then I have even greater news. My dearest love, Duncan is coming, here, tonight."

The lady smiles. "I've heard. Your messenger arrived earlier. Things are prepared for this evening. Do you know how long the king plans to say?"

"Only until tomorrow morning."

"Then that day will never come for him."

Macbeth grimaces as uncertainty runs through his mind. He starts to speak, but she places a raised index finger across his lips to still his voice.

"Your face, my lord, is like a book betraying your feelings. If we are to deceive them, you must appear how they expect you to look. I know this may seem a terrible thing, but we have no choice if fate has proclaimed it. We must lie with our good deeds while plan their falls behind our backs."

"My wife...."

"Greet the king with a welcoming in both words and expression. You should appear as innocent as a flower." Her voice drops menacingly. "But you will be the snake hiding under the flower. The king is coming, and fate demands we take care of this now. I will have everything prepared for you, dearest husband."

"Are you sure...."

She again cuts him off. "Everything will change after tonight. Our lives will be different, and for the better."

"This matter is not so easily decided upon, honored wife. We will speak about this further."

"Fine. We will talk, but do not look troubled lest you arouse suspicion of wrong doings. Leave everything else up to me."

Chapter 6

Two carriages move up the road toward the castle at Inverness with horse mounted handlers and soldiers as an escort. Trees give away to the field rising up to the hilltop on which the castle resides. Two lines of guardsmen stand abreast beside the road on both sides coming from the castle gates. Lady Macbeth stands just inside the gates, waiting at the head of a red carpet which has been rolled out over the road.

The first carriage pulls sideways to it, allowing the passengers to step out. Duncan is the first, followed by his sons. They appraise the castle as the second carriage drives up and lets out Banquo, Macduff, Angus, and Ross. The eight men begin to walk toward the castle as trumpeters begin playing the king's march.

Duncan gazes lovingly at the home of Macbeth. "This castle is such a pleasant place. The air is sweet and appeals to me."

Banquo steps close to the king. "The summer bird martin builds his nests here because of how inviting the breezes are. There isn't a single perch on the castle walls those birds haven't nested on. They always settle where the air is the nicest."

Lady Macbeth approaches the men. Duncan sees her and waves. "Look, gentlemen, here comes our honored hostess. I say, sometimes the love my subjects throw at me is entirely inconvenient, but I still accept it. In doing so, I teach all of you to thank me for the inconvenience I'm causing you. It is how I show my love to you all."

Lady Macbeth curtsies before the king, having heard the end of what he said. "Everything that we do for you, even if doubled, is nothing compared to the honor you bring us by enjoying our hospitality. We welcome you as our guest with much gratitude for the dignities you heap upon us."

Duncan nods to her. "Tell me, where is Macbeth, the Thane of Cawdor? We followed closely after he departed. I hoped to arrive before him, but he rides so swiftly. It must have been his great love in returning home that spurred his haste to beat us here."

"I am a lucky woman, my lord, to have such a devoted husband."

"Indeed you are doubly lucky, for we are to be your guests tonight."

She feigns surprise at his words. "Then we shall be your servants, your highness. Everything of our home is at your disposal, for after all, we keep it in trust only and would give you back everything that is yours," Lady Macbeth says.

The king replies, "Give me your hand, fair lady, and lead me to my host. I love him dearly, and I wish to continue my favor to him. When you are ready, hostess."

"It would be my pleasure. This way, please." She leads the men into the castle, to the dining hall.

Macbeth is there waiting for them. When the king enters, a flourish of servants start bringing in trays upon trays of food, placing them over the giant table. "If it will please you, my king, please join me in our humble feast in your honor."

Chapter 7

Macbeth paces down an empty hall, far away from the bustle of the dinner his house honors the king with. His manservant Seyton stands at the doors entrance, making sure nobody interrupts his lord's ramblings.

Macbeth talks to himself like a man possessed. "If this business would really be done with this single deed, then I would get it over with quickly. If merely assassinating Duncan would sweep everything away and prevent any consequences when I'm named king, I would gladly put my immortal soul and the next word at risk to have it done. But what I am thinking? Surely the consequences that would come in this world would be dire. I may just be making myself a target to rogue upstarts who would be king. Justice would have me drink from the same poisoned glass that I would serve the king. Just like Macdonwald, and the former Cawdor."

He reaches the end of the corridor and turns around to continue marching back toward Seyton, chewing over his thoughts. "The king trusts me two fold. First, I am his kinsman and subject, so I should always try to protect him. Secondly, I'm his host, so I should be the one protecting him from murder, not trying to do him in myself." He throws his hands into the air. "This is crazy. Duncan is such a humble leader, so free of corruption that he will leave behind a great legacy, and surely angels will play trumpets to the injustice of his untimely death. The news of this will disperse on the wind to spread the horrible deed to all corners of the realm. A veritable flood of tears will be shed at his loss."

Macbeth stops marching and declares, "I can't push myself to act. Only ambition motivates me, and by itself it would have me rushing ahead into disaster."

The door at the end of the corridor opens. Seyton allows the person through, and Macbeth sees it is his wife. She walks up to him, leaving the other to continue watching the doorway.

Macbeth asks, "Do you have any news?"

She replies briskly while approaching, "He has almost finished his dinner. Why did you leave early?"

"Did he ask for me?"

She exclaims, "You haven't heard that he has?" She stops in front of her husband.

"We can't do this. The king has just honored us greatly. The power we are going to gain already is significant. I want to enjoy these honors and not throw them away so soon."

She sneers at him. "Were you drunk before? You were willing to kill him earlier."

"I said we would need to talk further."

She says, "Did you go to sleep and wake up green with fear? Is this how I should remember your love to me? Do you not wish to give me the world?"

"How can your words be so cruel?"

"Why are you afraid to act how you desire? Will you take the crown you want so badly, or just live like a coward?"

"Please, stop! Why are you so callus? I only wish to do what is proper for a man of my stature. Those who dare do more are not men at all."

"If you were not a man when you told me you wished to do this in the first place, then what manner of beast were you? It must have been a beast willing to take care of its wife. No. If you dared to go even further, you'd be that much more of a man."

Macbeth flinches back as if struck. "You call me a coward, and then you question my manhood. Did I not just lead the kingdom into victory against two great foes with nary a scratch to show for it?"

She coldly asks, "What of it?"

"I may have fallen, to not come back and feel your embrace again. Yet you do not bask in that great fortune even for a moment before whisking it aside. There is honor in living in the present, my wife."

She pokes at his chest with a manicured fingernail. "You are the one who wished to do this. But now that the time is perfect, it is almost too good for you. I have suckled a baby and know the sweetness of that love, but I would have plucked my nipple from its mouth and smashed its head against a wall if I had sworn to do so as eagerly as you sworn to become the king."

"But if we fail...."

"If we fail? If you would just find the courage to stand for your family, we will not. Our plan is perfect. When Duncan is asleep, which after that meal and a hard day's journey will be soon, I'll be a good hostess and get his servants so drunk that they won't remember anything. And when they sleep like pigs, drunk and dead to the world, Duncan will be unguarded and asleep himself. Whatever happens then will be blamed on the servants."

"My wife," Macbeth says in utter shock at his wife's ruthlessness. "May you only give birth to males, because your fearless spirit could create nothing that isn't masculine."

"How sweet of you. And what are we going to do to make sure the servants are to blame?"

"Wife...."

"What are you going to do?" she insists.

"We will cover the servants with blood after using their daggers to kill the king. But what if someone does not believe they killed the king?"

"Who would think it was anything else? We'll be grieving with everyone when we hear of Duncan's death. Now, are you ready to do this? Are you ready to show me how much you love me?"

Resignation in his voice, Macbeth replies, "Yes, wife. I will make every muscle in my body move to carry this out." He raises her hand to his lips and kisses it. "Go now, and pretend to be a friendly hostess. Hide what you know we plan. They cannot know, or Duncan may not be the one to miss the next sunrise."

"As you say, my thane."

Book 2

Chapter 1

Tired of tossing and turning under his sheets, Banquo sits up, annoyed with himself. His mind will not find peace with the events of the past couple weeks rampaging through his thoughts. All of the dead bodies, most of them his countrymen, many of which were his friends. They march through his mind and keep sleep at bay. Their dead eyes gaze at him, accusing him of surviving as he led them to their deaths.

Banquo understands the necessity of the warfare though. The world is a deadly place, but if it is not stood up against, the danger would be magnitudes higher. All of these lives are spent in place of tens of thousands more that suffer if left unchecked. The killing is a sin, but not killing would be a greater sin, to turn his back on the needs of the crown. And losing one's life is the price a soldier may pay.

But even then, it is not the battles of the past couple weeks to which his mind keeps returning. The dead are merely a side note to the memory of the three witches. They foretold of the king's death, and revolution. Would Macbeth strive to reach such a lofty goal? Banquo did not know, but he does know his friend's ambition. And now Macbeth and the king both sleep under the same roof.

Banquo stands from his bed and pads barefoot to the door, where he grabs his sword and belt, strapping it over his hip. He slips his feet into his boots and steps out of the room without tying the laces. He walks the halls feeling lost in his thoughts, uncertain of where he walks but trying to find content in the darkness breathing the cool night air. He treads from one hall to another, eventually opening a door that leads onto a catwalk overlooking the courtyard below. He lets out a deep, world-weary sigh as he steps outside feeling slightly better.

The catwalk curves away, and once on it, he can see someone else is already here, holding a torch, looking off into the night. Banquo smiles, seeing it is his son Fleance.

As he walks over, Banquo calls out, "How fair is the night, son?"

Fleance does not look his way when he replies, "It's dark. The moon has set, but I haven't heard the clock strike yet."

"The moon sets at twelve, doesn't it?"

"I think it's much later than that, father. Nearing morning, I would guess."

"Is it?" Banquo asks, uninterested. "I suppose you are having trouble finding sleep just like your old man?"

Fleance grunts his reply.

Banquo stands beside the other. "The heavens are stingy with its light tonight. The rain left but forgot many of its clouds." He stretches and yawns, placing his hands down on the ledge as he looks over the courtyard. Trying to get comfortable, he pulls his sword and belt off. "Here. Do your old man a favor. Take my sword. I feel so tired and heavy. Merciful powers, I beg you to keep the nightmares out of my thoughts and allow sleep to take me."

Fleance grabs the blade, and the two men stand there for minutes, neither speaking. Both are lost in their heavy thoughts, so when a light comes into view, it makes them start in fright, the tranquility dispelled.

Quietly to his son, Banquo commands, "Fleance, give me my sword back." He takes the blade out of the scabbard his son still holds and calls out "Who approaches?"

A voice drifts over to them "It is I, Macbeth, kind Banquo."

Torch light shows the Thane of Cawdor and a servant

approaching across the catwalk.

"Macbeth? You're not yet at rest, sir? The king is asleep."

"I suppose he would be."

"Indeed." Banquo stares quizzically at the other man before jumping as he remembers something he was bidden to do. "Oh, Duncan did bid me to give this to you." He reaches into his pocket and pulls out something he keeps hidden in his hand. "Duncan has been in an unusually good mood. He has already granted so many gifts to your household and servants. You are most fortunate."

"I only do as I should. I am grateful to be able to show my gratitude to the king."

"And now he wishes this." Banquo stretches his hand out, placing a giant diamond in Macbeth's hand. "It is a present to your wife for her measureless hospitality."

Macbeth seems to dismiss the giant diamond. "We were so unprepared for the king's visit. We couldn't entertain him as well as we would want to."

"You seem distracted tonight, my friend. Worry not, for everything is well. I dreamt of the three witches again, as I'm sure you probably did as well. They will not leave my wandering mind free to sleep, but they at least told you part of the truth."

Macbeth glances at Fleance, and then looks back to his friend. "I don't waste any time thinking about them. But if you want, we can discuss the matter later, time permitting."

"Whenever it's convenient for you."

Macbeth moves up to him and whispers in his ear. "If you remain my friend by my side, when the time comes, there will be great honor coming to you."

Whispering back, Banquo says, "I'll be there for you as long as you don't ask me to do something that I cannot do on a clear conscience."

"Then rest easily in the mean time," Macbeth says as he steps back.

"Thank you, sir. And the same to you. Sleep well."

Banquo and his son take their leave, walking off the catwalk and back into the castle. Macbeth watches them until the door closes. He looks down, seeing a bench against the catwalk's wall and stares down at it as a ray of moonlight pierces the clouds.

Still looking down at the bench as if the most interesting thing in the world is stashed there, he says to the servant, "You may go and get some rest yourself. Oh, but before that, please tell your mistress to strike the bell when my drink is ready."

The servant bows. "Thank you, my lord." He leaves, heading through the same door Banquo disappeared through, leaving Macbeth alone, in the dark.

The Thane of Cawdor continues to stare down at the bench in the darkness. The moon shines over his shoulder and down on the bench. It reflects off of a piece of metal, round and engraved, hidden under the seat, most likely cast aside. Macbeth bends down to get a better look.

"What is a dagger doing here?" He reaches for it, noticing the handle faces him, angled to be grasped easily. "It's almost like it was put here just for me." He reaches forward but stops his hand before grabbing it. "It must be a hallucination, born of my stressed mind. It cannot be so easy. A dagger placed for me, so close to the king's chamber. Surely it cannot be fated that I murder Duncan. Can that really be our entwined fates?" He looks off to the far door of the catwalk, where the king's room rests only down the hallway beyond. He turns back to the dagger. "I can see you. But can I touch you? Are you more than the stress of my mind?"

Macbeth grabs the handle and picks the dagger up. "I was already heading that way, but here I find you, placed to make sure I don't falter perhaps? I was going to use a weapon just like you, taken from one of the king's servants." He stands, cradling the dagger as he would a child. "Is that blood already staining you? Why didn't I see that before?" He looks away. "There isn't really a dagger, is there? It's made from my fevered mind. The stress placed this hallucination here, putting the murder outside of me. I'm not to be blamed."

He takes a step back and looks out across the courtyard, where he first saw Banquo. "Half of the world is asleep and dreaming of evil things. Like witches, sacrificing people to their vile goddess. Dreams of old men being murdered, roused by the cries of wolves, walking to his death as quietly as one already dead."

His eyes begin to water. "Please, don't allow my feet to step toward his lone walk. It will happen on its own if it was meant to be. Duncan lives now, and I am not going to be the one to change that. How could I?"

A bell rings out, making Macbeth jump in fright, clenching the handle of the knife tight to his chest. "Even the bell is telling me to push Duncan off of the mortal coil." He shakes his head. "Don't listen to the bell. Don't listen to the bell!"

Macbeth looks back to the door. Floating before it is a dagger exactly like the one he holds. It points toward the door. Macbeth steps to it, but it moves forward, passing through the door. "It goes to Duncan, much like the funeral bells I hear. The bells summon you to the afterlife, my king. I will save you."

****

The room is dark as the only light is the slight glow from the moon shining in through a curtained window. Everything is still and silent save the quiet breathing of the sleeping man. He lays on the large bed in the room's center. Macbeth steps across the chamber, ever so slowly, worried each pace will creak and give away his presence.

The servants are asleep in a drunken stupor outside the room. The king is alone. All is how it should be. But should it be? Should the king die this night?

Macbeth steps closer, cautiously, inching up next to the bed. The old man sleeps there under the covers, his eyes close and mouth open with a slight snore. Macbeth slides onto the bed, leaning over Duncan. The Thane of Cawdor raises his right hand up, gripping the dagger so tightly his knuckles turn white and begins aching.

Duncan still breathes despite the prophecy. Macbeth leans closer. He sees no danger to the king. The monarch's chest rises and falls steadily with each breath, but he otherwise does not move.

Macbeth leans even closer in, stopping with their noses mere inches apart.

A slickness of sweat forms on the thane's forehead, and it tickles as it runs down his nose, threatening to drip off of his flesh and land on the king's. Macbeth holds his breath, not wanting to give his presence away to the king, but he wants to be here, to watch as the king dies. Surely it will happen at any second. The witches said it would happen. Their dark goddess promised it.

The bead of sweat gathering on his nose pulls down, elongating, until it snaps loose and hits the king's nose. Duncan's eyes snap open. His pupils contract quickly, and fright shows in how wide his eyes stay. Moving on reflex, Macbeth slaps his hand over the king's mouth to stifle any shout he may release. Fright turns to confusion in Duncan's eyes.

Macbeth shushes the king to keep him quiet and he places the tip of the dagger against Duncan's chest, between two ribs. The king tries to shove the thane off, but the younger man's strength is unmovable. Macbeth pushes the dagger, piercing the tip through thin, aged flesh. A trickle of blood immediately flows around the blade's tip.

Macbeth pushes harder, but it does not take much strength as the blade is sharpened for battle. It slides through the old flesh with almost no resistance. The chest wall muscles flex around the blade, pulling it in Macbeth's hand, inadvertently changing where it plunges deep.

The king struggles further, thrashing about, kicking his legs, flaying his arms, but Macbeth will not be unseated from on top of him. The blade cuts through Duncan's aorta, and blood spurts from the incision, covering the thane and seeping between their bodies that are pressed together as lovers would be.

Their eyes stay locked on each other, and Macbeth keeps shushing the king. The thrashing all but stops as the eyes lose focus, and muffled shouts no longer try to arise from behind the iron grip of Macbeth's hand.

The Thane of Cawdor slowly rises off the old man, leaving the dagger in his chest, up to nearly the hilt. The king does not breathe or move. Macbeth steps back, staring. He says quietly to himself, "And so the days of Duncan, king, have passed."

From somewhere behind Macbeth, a voice cries out, "Murder!"

Chapter 2

An owl screeches into the twilight, making Lady Macbeth start in fright. "That owl shrieks like the bells rung during an execution. My lord Macbeth must be killing the king right now."

She paces back and forth in an inner chamber of the Macbeth's private rooms, ringing her hands together. "The servants are drunk and asleep with all the drugs I put into their drinks. They sleep so deeply I'm not so certain if they are alive or dead. What if they are dead? It would be hard for them to kill the king then. But the same liquor that made them drunk has so embolden me. Shame on them. Those drunk servants make a mockery of their jobs, leaving them snoring instead of protecting the king."

She stops pacing. "What if they were just faking? They know! They are awake, waiting for Macbeth."

She starts pacing again, looking down and shaking her head. "To attempt murdering the king and not succeeding would ruin us! We would be the ones executed."

A noise draws her attention, back to the chamber's door. She stands staring, holding her breath. When nothing further happens, she continues talking. "I put the servant's dagger where Macbeth would find it. He couldn't have missed it." She paces once again. "I shouldn't have left it to him. I would have done the deed myself if Duncan hadn't looked like my father when he was sleeping. Oh, my dear thane, where are you?"

The door slams open, nearly knocking Lady Macbeth from

her feet in fright. Macbeth walks through the door, carrying a dagger. His clothes are drenched in the slick stickiness of blood.

"My husband!" she exclaims, grateful to see him.

"I have done it. The deed is done." He stops, looking behind him. "Did you hear a noise?"

"I heard the owl scream."

He turns back to her. "When?"

"Just now."

"As I came down?"

Lady Macbeth answers, "Yes."

His eyes dart about as he thinks, and his wife stays across the room, seemingly stuck in place. He asks her, "Who was in the second chamber?"

"Donalbain and Malcolm, the king's sons."

Macbeth's eyes drop to his bloody hand that still holds the dagger. "This is such a sorry sight."

She clicks her tongue at him. "That's a stupid thing to say. We have succeeded."

His eyes catch her and holds her tight. "One of the servants cried out 'murder' in his sleep, and another laughed. I listened to them, unable to move. They said their prayers and went back to sleep."

"Then all is well." She finally moves to him but keeps her distance as he is covered in the king's blood.

"One servant cried 'God bless us!' The other said 'Amen.' It was as if they knew, as if they could see these bloody hands of mine."

"Don't be silly."

"I heard them well, wife. Their voices were frightened. And I couldn't say 'amen' with them when they said 'God bless us.'"

"It would have been foolish to do so. Don't think about it."

Macbeth says, "But why couldn't I say it? I am in such dire needing of God's blessing, but I couldn't say 'amen.'"

"Dear husband. We can't think that way about these deeds, lest it drives us crazy."

Macbeth continues as if he did not heed her. "I thought I

heard a voice cry out, saying 'Sleep no more. Macbeth is murdering sleep.' Innocent sleep. Sleep that soothes away the troubles of the heart and weariness of body. Sleep that heals the mind. It is the main nourishment in life's feast. And I have killed it!"

Lady Macbeth snaps, "What are you talking about?"

"I heard a voice cry out after the king's heart stopped. 'Sleep no more! Macbeth has murdered sleep, and therefore Cawdor shall sleep no more. Macbeth shall not sleep again.'"

"My worthy thane, you weaken yourself thinking such thoughts. You are no coward, and that's a coward's thought. Put it out of your mind." She at last reaches forward and touches her husband, forcing him to turn, and pushes him. "You must get some water and clean yourself up. If you are seen like this, there will be no doubt about who killed the king."

"Listen to me! Don't you understand what I'm saying?"

She continues without pausing. "And why did you bring that dagger with you? It has to remain in the king's chambers. Take it back. Oh, and while you are there, smear the guards with blood."

He spins, turning back to her, his eyes wide open. "I can't go back! I'm afraid to even think of what I've done. I cannot stand to look upon my deeds anymore."

"You are a coward!" she chastises him. "It is just your hallucinations. You always get them when under stress. But fine. Then give me the dagger. The dead king and passed out guards can't hurt you more than a picture can. Only children fear scary pictures. I'll smear the guards with blood as well. They must look guilty or someone may snoop around. And who knows what will be found then."

Lady Macbeth grabs the knife from his numb grasp and marches out of the room. He watches her go, unmoving, unbelieving what he did this night. The king is dead, by his hand no less, all brought on by the prophecy of witches of dark gods.

He hears a knocking and flinches. "What is that!" he exasperates. Macbeth closes his eyes and steadies his breathing. "What has happened to me? Jumping at every noise." He looks down to his hands. "Are these hands really mine? Were they always so stained with blood? I don't think all of the water in the oceans can wash them clean. My hands will surely stain the seas crimson." He sits, staring at his hands. Macbeth does not know how long he sits there, staring at his blooded hands.

Lady Macbeth reenters the room. She looks for her husband, and upon seeing him, she scoffs. "What is becoming of you? You are to be king! Rejoice."

He raises his hands to show her.

"What? My hands are as bloodied as yours, but I would be ashamed if my heart was so weak as yours."

The knocking comes again.

"That must be the south entrance. Come with me." She offers her blood covered hand to Macbeth. "Let's retire to our chamber." She kneels before him, looking into his downcast eyes. "A little water is all that is needed to wash away all evidence. How easy it is to be freed from guilt. You have lost your resolve. Come with me and we will find it again."

The knocking booms out.

"My husband, snap out of your daze!"

"I would rather be unconscious than think of what I have done."

Again the knocking carries through the room.

Macbeth snaps, "Knock and knock again. Wake Duncan. I wish the knocking would bring you back to consciousness."

Lady Macbeth sighs. She stands back up and reaches down to take his hand and pulls him to his feet. "Let's go, my husband."

Chapter 3

"Knocking and knocking. And knocking again," slurs the porter. "Why is there so much knocking? It's like I was the porter of hell, letting poor souls in at all hours, and a constant stream of them at that!"

The rapping on the door comes again as he stumbles toward the south gate.

"Knock, knock, knock! Who's there, coming to my door in the devil's name? Is it a farmer who hanged himself, finding his grain was worth but a tithe of what he thought? Oh yes, it is the farmer! Just as I thought." He bows to an imaginary farmer. "Did you bring your handkerchief? You are going to need it. You will sweat a lot here."

Knocking again runs through the halls.

"Knock, knock! Who's there, in the devil's name? Maybe it's a con man who died after lying under oath. But you can't lie to God, can ya? You have been sent to hell for perjury, so come in, con man."

The banging on the southern entrance calls out again.

"Knock, knock, knock! In the devil's name, who's there? Are you a tailor looking to skimp on the fabric for clothes you were paid to make? Come on in, tailor."

The insistent knocking continues.

"Knock, knock! Can't you just be quiet? What are you? But I

guess this place is too cold to be hell. I am not a porter to the devil, am I? I suppose I should not let them into hell, but into our hall."

The knocking booms out, coming more and more impatient.

"I'm coming! I'm coming. Don't forget to tip the poor porter when he lets you in."

The drunken porter releases the latch and pulls the door. The gate swings open, showing Macduff and Lennox waiting on the other side.

Macduff scoffs, "Was it such a late night, my friend, that you had a hard time getting up this morning?"

The porter sways in his stance. "That's right, sir. We were partying till after 3 in the morning." He winks to the two men. "And I'm sure you know drink is a great provoker of three things."

"Oh really," Macduff prods the porter. "And what three things will drink cause a man to do?"

"It will turn your nose red." To illustrate, he tries to find his nose with his right index finger, but he has to try a couple times before finally finding it. "That's it. And!" he exclaims, "It makes you sleep all too long, and urinate. Both together, if you imbibe too much."

Lennox asks, "That's the three things?"

"I know what you think, good sirs," the porter says. "But while it provokes lust, it also unprovokes as well. I mean to say, it gives one the desire." he leans forward, whispering behind his hand as if imparting a great secret. "But it also hinders performance." He stands back up as straight as his unstable form allows, pointing his index to the ceiling. "Therefore, too much is like falling for a con. It sets you up, and then pulls the rug from under you before you even know it. You know? It gets you 'up,' but keeps you from getting off. It persuades you while discouraging you. Makes you stand at attention but takes it away when needed. What I'm trying to say is it makes you think the erotic but leaves you asleep and pissing yourself instead."

Macduff laughs. "My friend, I believe the drink did all of this to you last night. You need a bath."

"That it did, sir. It got me by the throat and would not let go.

But I was too strong for the drink. It weakened my legs, but I managed to cast it out! Yep, I also puked on myself."

Lennox gags, raising his hand to cover his nose and mouth.

Macduff asks, "Is your master awake?"

As if on key, Macbeth walks into the entry room.

"Ah!" Macduff exclaims. "Our knocking must have awakened him. Hail, Thane of Cawdor!"

Lennox says, "Good morning, noble sir."

Macbeth replies, "Good morning as well, to both of you."

"Is the king stirring yet, worthy thane?" Macduff asks.

"I'm afraid not as yet," Macbeth replies.

"Well, I must be off to see him," Macduff says. "He commanded me to wake him early. I've almost missed the hour he wished to rise."

"Then follow me, and I will bring you to him."

Macbeth turns and heads back the way he came, and the other two follow him. The porter watches them walk off before he nearly falls over. He rubs his red nose and stumbles away, muttering to himself, forgotten by the noble men.

Macduff says while following Macbeth, "I understand the burden the king can be despite the honor he places upon you. And yet you are still most gracious to lead me yourself."

"Maybe there is some burden in being the crown's host, but we take delight in providing for Duncan, as he provides for us with the honor of his presence," Macbeth replies.

He takes them directly to the king's chambers, foregoing the jaunt over the catwalk on the walls. He stops at the chamber door to the king's rooms. "This is it, good Macduff."

"Then if you will excuse me. I must perform my duty, however limited it is." Macduff opens the door and steps inside.

Lennox turns to Macbeth. "Is the king leaving today?"

"That he is. I was asked to arrange his passage."

Lennox stretches, putting his hands together over his head and arching his back while releasing a yawn. "Did you sleep well last night, worthy thane? The night was unruly for me. The wind howled down the chimney, and people said they heard strange screams in the air, screams of death. And terrible voices carried prophecies of dire and confused events that would hatch a woeful age. Some even said the ground shook." Lennox shrugs. "All I heard was the owl."

"It was a rough night," Macbeth confirms. He smiles then. "I too heard an owl though."

"I can't remember a single night like this. I would think the moon was full."

Macduff burst through the door, breathing hard. His eyes are as wide as saucers and his face flushed. "Oh, horror!" he shouts. "It is beyond words and belief."

"What's the matter?" Macbeth and Lennox ask together.

Macduff tries to calm himself long enough to answer. "The worst thing possible has happened. A murderer has stolen into your castle and took the life right out of it."

"What are you talking about?" Macbeth demands.

"Is the king okay?" Lennox asks.

"I can't even say. Go look for yourselves. I cannot find the strength to speak such evil."

Macbeth and Lennox hurry into the king's chambers. The hall is lined with four doors and ends at another. The doorway at the end gaps open, and the two hurry through to where the king sleeps. Lying on the bed is the body of the king, chest torn open from repeated stabbings, though little blood flowed from those wounds because he was already dead when those gashes were made. The sheets the body lays upon are turned deep crimson and glistening from the thickening blood. And the king's skin, where not spotted with the staining life giving blood, is ashen gray.

Lennox falls to his knees, crying out. "No! What monster could have done this?"

"I aim to find out," Macbeth says as he turns and marches from the room. The first door to the left is the guards' room. He throws the doorway open and steps inside, Lennox scrambling to follow him. On the floor lay the two guards. They snore deeply, and their arms and faces are plastered in blood. Though the men are on the floor, the beds are not empty. Upon their pillows lay the bloody daggers uses to kill the king.

Macbeth screams in rage, waking the guards in a fright. They both sit up, their eyes wide open in surprise. Macbeth pulls out his sword and levels it against one of their throats. That guard becomes still while the other leaps backward in uncertainty.

"What do you have to say for yourself, having committed this crime?" Macbeth demands.

"What crime?" the guard with the blade to his throat stutters.

The other guard looks his companion over and shouts, "You are covered in blood! Who's blood is on you?"

The other guard looks back at the other, trying to remain as still as possible with the blade pressed against his throat. "You are just as covered in blood."

"What?" He looks down as his hands. "Oh, dear God! What has happened?"

"You killed the king!" Macbeth roars.

Both look at him in utter shock. "But we...."

"Silence, murderer." Macbeth swipes with his blade, cutting deep into the first guard's throat. The man falls backward, covering his neck with his hands, trying to stint the blood, but his arms become too heavy and limp, and his body crumples sideways mere seconds later, his eyes staring into nothingness.

The second guard, having found the resolve to survive greater than that of the shock, leaps up and grabs the blood dagger from his bed. "I swear, upon my love for my king, I did no harm to Duncan!"

"Liar!" Macbeth screams and lunges forward. The guard makes to defend himself with his dagger, but the small blade cannot stop the thane's rage. The blade plunges deep into the guard's chest. Macbeth blinks in frozen thought as he watches the blade tip pierce the other's chest in precisely the same place as the dagger did into Duncan mere hours earlier. The guard falls to his knees, tears trailing down his face, clearing the blood from his cheeks. He tumbles over. As his body falls, Macbeth's blade is pulled from his chest.

From the hallway, Macbeth hears Macuff shouting, "Awake, awake! Ring the alarm bell for murder and treason. Banquo and Donalbain! Malcolm! Awake. Shake off your sleep that hold you like death and look upon death itself. Up, up, and see this great doom. Malcolm! Banquo! Rise up from your slumber and come see this horror. Why is that bloody bell not ringing yet?"

The bell begins to ring franticly as if Macduff rang it himself. He continues to shout, stopping only when Lady Macbeth enters. "What is this business? Why is the bell ringing and the trumpets playing to rise everyone from sleep in my house? Speak, Macduff."

"Oh gentle lady, this news is not for you to hear. I fear it would kill you as soon as I speak it."

One of the side doors open and Banquo enters, wiping away the sleep that still lingers in his eyes.

Macduff grabs the other's shoulders in both hands. "Oh Banquo. Banquo. Our king has been murdered."

"What?" Lady Macbeth demands. "Surely not in my home!"

Banquo goes to her side and wraps his arm around her shoulders to help steady her. "Dear lady, it would be too cruel an event regardless of where it occurred. But dear Macduff." He turns back to the lord. "Say it is not so, that you are giving a joke in the worst possible taste."

Macbeth comes back, and Lennox follows close behind. The Thane of Cawdor says, "If I had died only an hour ago, I would have thought I lived a blessed life. But now, what use have we to continue living? Everything is merely toys now, containing nothing real and of substance. The king is dead. The wine of his life has been poured out, leaving merely the waste behind."

Donalbain and Malcolm open the door of the room and step into the hallway. Ross enters from the last door. The three of them are anxious, seeing the panic the others are in.

Donalbain demands, "What is amiss?"

Macbeth looks to the king's sons and replies, "You are amiss but don't even know it yet. The source of the spring of your royal blood has stopped."

Donalbain and Malcolm look to each other, not

understanding but looking for comprehension in the other.

Macduff answers their unspoken question. "Your royal father is murdered."

Malcolm demands in a sprung fit of rage, "Who did it!"

Sounding subdued against the prince's outrage, Lennox says, "It seems it was his guards protecting the chamber. They are covered with blood, and their daggers we found on their pillows were covered in the royal blood as well. They acted like they were confused. We should not have trusted anyone's life to them."

Macbeth looks down. "I killed them for their deeds. I still feel the regret of my lashing out."

Macduff is confused. "Why did you do that?"

The Thane of Cawdor looks pained. "Is it possible to be wise, bewildered, calm and furious, loyal and neutral all in the same moment? I don't think any man can. I was overtaken by violent love for Duncan. It caused me to act irrationally before I could give myself pause. I could only see the face of Duncan, his milky skin covered in his precious blood. The stab wounds looked like a breach of nature. And there, near him, I found the murderers, dripping with his blood. Their daggers were covered with the gore of their foul deeds. Who could have refrained from taking vengeance? Surely not anyone who loved Duncan enough with the courage to act upon it."

Lady Macbeth stumbles in apparent weakness. "Somebody help me."

"Look to the lady," Macduff commands.

The men gather around her and help her to the ground as she faints. Servants rush in around Lady Macbeth while the men step back, and they carry her limp form off.

Banquo then says, "None of us are dressed properly for the cold of the day. Let's get ourselves presentable and meet in the hall to discuss this bloody crime and figure out what happened. We're all shaken up by fears and doubts. I am putting myself into God's hands to find the secrets out that plotted the treasonous killing of dear Duncan."

Macduff says, "So will I."

"And I," the others agree in unison.

Macbeth says, "Then let's dress quickly and meet in the hall as suggested."

The men leave the hallway, all except Malcolm and Donalbain, who stand staring at each other.

Malcolm breaks the silence. "We can't stay with them. It is too easy for a liar to pretend to feel sorrow when he feels none. Where are you going? I'm heading to England."

Donalbain nods in accent. "We will both be safer if we go separate ways. I will go to Ireland. Remember, dear brother, that wherever we go, men will smile at us with daggers hidden behind their backs ready to end our lives. Those closest to us will be more likely to murder us. Only such a person would have the desire to do away with our father, to clear a path to the throne."

"We have not yet seen where the danger comes from, so it would be best to avoid it entirely. It would be prudent to find our horses and not worry about polite goodbyes. We must flee quickly lest we find no mercy for our lives here anymore."

Donalbain says, "Ride fast, brother. Watch your back."

"And to you."

Chapter 4

Ross sits in the courtyard, pondering all that he had already heard. An old man comes up and sits next to him. "I can remember these past seventy years. There were hours of dreadful and strange happenings, but the horrors of last night makes everything that has come before merely a bad joke."

"You can see the sky even looks upset with the actions of mankind, for they are threatening the ground with their storms. The clock says it is day, but the darkness of night lingers, strangling the sun. I can't even guess if it is because the night was so strong, or the day feels so weak. But darkness still entombs the world even though it should be bright."

"It is unnatural, just like the deeds of last night. Last Tuesday, a falcon was circling high up, but it was killed by an owl that normally hunts mice."

Ross says, "And you know, something else strange happened. Duncan's horses are the most beautiful and swift, the best of their breeds, but they turned wild and broke out of their stalls. They were obstinate as if making war with mankind."

The old man says, "I heard the horses actually ate each other. Have you ever heard of such a thing?"

"I would not believe it if I didn't see it with my own two eyes. It is true." They fall silent, thinking of the end of days that surely must be coming.

Macduff enters the courtyard and prods over to Ross. "How are things going?" Ross asks.

Macduff wipes a tear away from his eye. "Isn't the answer to that apparent enough?"

Ross drops his eyes. "What I meant to ask was if we know who committed this horrible deed?"

"We can't figure anything out other than it was the servants that Macbeth executed."

"Too bad he did that, really," Ross says. "What good would it have done to kill those men?"

Macduff scowls at Ross. "They were paid to kill their master. They did not deserve to live! And now, Malcolm and Donalbain, the king's own sons, have fled. What can we believe other than they are the masterminds of this tragedy?"

Ross says, "Everything about this seems unnatural. What stupid ambition for a son to kill his father, especially one that supports him. Sovereignty will fall upon Macbeth then, I suppose."

"Already happened. He has been named king and has left for Scone to be crowned."

"And where is Duncan's body?"

"Carried to Colmekill, to be put in the tomb of his ancestors, to hopefully find peace in the afterlife."

Ross asks, "Are you going to Scone then?"

"No, cousin, I'm going home to Fife."

"I suppose I will go to Scone myself then." Ross stands. "Farewell, old man," he says to the gentleman he was talking with.

"May God's blessing go with you and those who would turn bad into good and foe into friends."

Book 3

Chapter 1

Banquo is walking through the grand palace of Scone, just outside of Perth, where the Scottish King is crowned. He moves down the long gallery on the red carpet, under the arched ceiling. One wall of this hall is interspaced with nearly floor to ceiling windows, and the other wall contains many masterful works of art. Paintings hang on the walls, pottery is setting on display cases, and busts perch on pedestals.

All of the art is lost on Banquo in his ravings. "You have it all now, don't you? Cawdor, Glamis, and now all of Scotland. It's as the witches promised. And I am most certain you cheated most foully to achieve it. I wonder what deeds it took to gain your two thaneships. And yet it was said it will not be your descendants that will be future kings. That will be my honor. My sons and grandsons. That is if the witches tell the truth, but they sure did for you."

A trumpet plays, silencing Banquo's musings. He turns to see Macbeth walking down the gallery toward him with Lady Macbeth beside him, both dressed in royal plumage. Coming behind them are numerous lords and ladies, Lennox and Ross among them, as are Menteith and Caithness. And farther still are their numerous attendants. Just behind Macbeth is his ever present manservant Seyton.

Macbeth indicates toward Banquo. "And here's our most important guest."

Lady Macbeth says, "If he had been forgotten, then our celebration would be incomplete. I cannot allow that and still be a gracious hostess."

Macbeth stops before Banquo and grips his friend's shoulder. "Tonight we will hold a ceremonial banquet, sir, and I request your presence."

Banquo bows. "If your highness commands it of me, it shall be my duty as always."

Macbeth asks, "Are you going riding this afternoon?"

"Yes, my good lord."

"I wish I had your good advice today at council as your words have always been honest and helpful, but I suppose that will have to wait until tomorrow then. How far will you ride today?"

"I plan to ride a ways. I shan't be back until dinner I expect. Unless my horse borrows its speed from the night herself, I will not be back but an hour or two after twilight."

"Just don't miss our feast. I would not take that well."

Banquo says, "My lord, I wouldn't miss it for my life."

Macbeth steps aside, pulling Banquo with him. He whispers, "I hear the princes, our murderous cousins, have hidden in England and Ireland. They haven't confessed murdering their honored father and have been telling all sort of strange lies. But we can talk of that tomorrow, when we discuss matters of state that affect both of us." He stands back and says loud enough for the others to hear, "Hurry to your horse. Goodbye until tonight." He turns to leave but then stops after taking half a step. He turns back to the other. "Is Fleance riding with you today?"

Banquo stares at Macbeth, seeing cold calculations in his eyes. He tries to hide his shudder. "Yes, my good lord." He swallows hard. "It's time we get going."

Macbeth smiles. "I hope your horses are fast and surefooted. And with that, farewell, my friend."

Banquo takes a few steps backward, keeping his eyes on the new king before turning and all but running down the hall.

When he disappears from the gallery, Macbeth says," Everybody may go as they see fit until seven tonight. To keep your time yours, I will make myself scarce until suppertime. Until then, God be with you."

Everyone files away, leaving Macbeth alone, all save Seyton. "Are those men waiting for me?"

He answers, "Yes, my lord. They wait your words outside the palace gate."

"Bring them to me."

The servant bows and departs without a further word.

Macbeth turns to the nearest window and looks out it, leaning forward on one hand placed on the wall. There are a couple kids kicking a ball back and forth outside. "Being king means nothing if I'm not safe. I am afraid of Banquo. There is nobility in his actions that I fear. He dares to take risks, and his tempered mind never stops. He has the wisdom to act both bravely and safely."

He stands straight and looks back at the art in the gallery. "There is nobody I fear but him. He demanded of the witches his own future. And they named his line that of kings, not mine. They gave me the crown and scepter but then promised I will not pass it on to my heir. No son of mine will wear the crown. If this is true, then murdering Duncan was a gracious act for Banquo's sons." He smashes his fist on the wall. "I ruined my peace for their benefit. I gave my eternal soul to the devil to make another man's sons kings! Banquo's sons! Kings! I rather not see that fate come about. I will challenge fate and battle it to death if need be."

A sound comes down the hall. "Who's there?" he booms out.

"I have returned with the men you desired to speak with," Seyton answers.

"Very well," Macbeth calls.

Macbeth looks over the two men, nodding his head in acceptance that he chose right. They carry no weapons as they are not allowed in the palace save for the guardsmen, but the king can see even under the heavy capes they wear thick leather, not quite leather, but still strong enough to provide protection while allowing them to move swiftly.

Macbeth asks of them, "Wasn't it just yesterday that we

spoke to each other?"

The first man replies, "It was, your highness."

"Very well. Did you consider what I said then? It was Banquo who made your lives hard for so long when you thought it was I. I showed you the proof of this yesterday, how you were deceived. Only a half-wit would not see how Banquo is to blame."

The first man says, "You explained it well yesterday."

"Then I just must know, why are you so patient and forgiving of Banquo? Why do you let go of his deeds? Is it that you are so pious to pray for this man and his children, whose heavy hand pushes you all to an early grave by forcing unending poverty on you?"

"We are but men, my liege. There is only so much we can do."

"Yes, you are a part of the species called man. Just as hounds, and greyhounds, mongrels, spaniels, mutts, shaggy lapdogs, swimming dogs, and wolf dogs are all dogs. Each dog can be listed according to their value of their breeds for being fast or slow, clever, and those that make good watchdogs and hunters. Each can be classified according to their natural gifts that separate them from all other dogs. It is the same with men. Each of us has a station in the file. If your place is not at the very bottom, then tell me now. Because if that is the case, I will tell you a plan to be rid of your enemy and raise your station closer to mine."

The second man asks, "And why would you share this with us?"

Macbeth growls, "As long as Banquo is alive, I will remain sick. I will only be healthy when he breaths no more."

"My liege, I am one such man. I've been kicked around by the world, and I'm so angry that I do not concern myself with what the world would do with me."

The first man says, "And I am the same. I'm so weary from disasters and bad luck that I'd risk my very life for any chance to fix my life once and for all, be it either made better or over."

Macbeth glares at them. "Both of you know Banquo is your enemy who stands between you and a better life, a higher station."

"It is true, my lord."

"He is my enemy too," Macbeth says. "His life is such a disturbance in mine that every minute of his living eats away at my heart. But alas!" He sits on a chair against the wall as if too exasperated to remain standing. "I have the power to do away with him, to sweep him from this life, but I cannot. He and I share many friends that I need to rely upon, so I have to be able to show my despair over his loss, which I can't do if I am known to have killed him. That is why I need your assistance. The eyes of the public cannot know I was involved in any way, for it would weigh heavy upon my work."

The second man says, "We shall perform as you command us, my lord."

The first says, "Though our lives…."

Macbeth cuts him off. "Your determination shines through your eyes. I will advise you where to hide yourselves and when to strike. It has to be done tonight and away from the palace. I must remain free from suspicion regardless of what happens. For the plan to work, Banquo and his son Fleance must both fall this day. His son is just as much to blame for our problems as his father, perhaps even more so." He stands back up. "I will contact you both in an hour. Take this time to make sure you are willing to do what must be done."

"I have decided, my lord," the first says. "I will do as you ask."

"As will I," the second answers.

"Then stay inside the palace. I will summon you soon. Seyton, take these two men to a chamber where they will go unnoticed." After they are gone, Macbeth says quietly to himself, "The deal is closed, dear Banquo, my friend. If only you would stand beside me instead of before me. This night, your soul will make the trip to heaven."

Chapter 2

Lady Macbeth sits in the state drawing room, next to the fire place, listening to the wood popping. The blue carpets reaches to each wall with a golden circular design stitched in the middle, and a chandelier dangles above her head.

As the servant bows, she asks, "Has Banquo left the court?"

"Aye, madam, but he will return tonight."

"Tell my lord husband I would enjoy his company for a few words."

"I will do as you request, madam." The servant departs.

She remains in silent contemplation after the servant leaves. She wonders if everything they have gambled, which is their very lives, was for nothing. If Macbeth and she have gained everything at the cost of tranquility, to have everything but peace, then they have gained nothing. It would be better to be the ones murdered than to be the murderer at the sacrifice of serenity.

Macbeth walks into the room, shattering her thoughts.

Lady Macbeth says to him, "What are you doing, keeping yourself hidden away with only your sad thoughts as company? Those thoughts should have been slain with the men they are about. Any worry without a remedy should be disregarded as there is no purpose to worry about that which you cannot fix. What is done is done."

"I have merely hurt the snake, not killed it. She will heal, and we will be in danger again. Heaven and Earth can fall apart and crumble before I'll abide eating our meals and sleeping in fear of the terrible affliction of my nightmares. I would much rather be dead and have peace than undergo such endless torment. Duncan is in his grave and sleeping well without life's troubles upon him. We have already done the worst thing that could afflict him, but nothing can harm him further."

"My gentle lord, come and relax with me. Smooth your harried face and be bright and jovial among your guests tonight."

Macbeth looks at her with a raised eyebrow. "That is what I intend to do, my love, and I pray you do the same."

"Of course I shall. Why would you ask that of me?"

"Give your special attention to Banquo this night. Talk to him and look at him in ways that will make him feel important. We are in danger, and we must flatter him to hide our true feelings and keep him unsuspicious."

She stands and steps deliberately toward him. "You must stop talking like this."

"Oh, it is like a poison in my mind, dear wife. You know Banquo and Fleance still live."

"But they can't forever."

"And I too find comfort in that thought," Macbeth agrees. "They can be killed. So be jovial. Before the bat flies tonight and the beetle hums in the evening, the dreadful deed will be done."

"Really?" She places her hand on her chest in surprise. "What are you going to do?"

"My sweet, innocent wife. It is best you do not know, so you can applaud it." He looks through one of the windows. "I wish night would hasten its arrival to blindfold the kind day and use its bloody and invisible hand to stop his heart and tear his body to pieces, to release my fear." His voice trails off, no longer talking to his wife. "The sky darkens, and the crows are returning to the woods. The good things of the day are beginning to sleep while the night's predators are arising to hunt." He looks back at his wife. "You marvel at my words, but do not question me. The bad things we have done demand more bad deeds. So please, come with me and appear happy. After all, you are the queen, my lady."

Lost in wonder at her husband's new found cruelty, she walks with him, hand in hand to the dining hall.

Chapter 3

The two men that met with Macbeth earlier this day stand hidden behind bushes trimmed into a wall along the path. They are on the palace grounds between the stables at the ground's wall and the gate into the palace. They have been hiding there for more than an hour when a third man approached them. They argue in hushed voices, fearful the sound would carry beyond their concealment.

The first man demands, "But who told you to come here and join us?"

The third man replies, "It was Macbeth."

The second says, "He was giving the same orders we were. Our lord wants us to work with him. Why else would he send another?"

The first scoffs. "Because he doesn't trust us to carry out this task. I will do as commanded."

The third replies, "As will I. Do you think you were the only one hurt by Banquo and his misdeeds? My family too has suffered greatly."

The first sighs. "Fine. Then stand with us and be our kin, but do not tarry when we must act. We are committed to this path, and so must you be if you will stand with us."

"Aye," the second agrees.

"And so I shall," the third answers.

The first man nods his accent before turning back to the

roadway. "Daylight has yet to completely be chased away by the night. Late travelers are hurrying to reach their inns for the night. Banquo should be passing by soon."

The third man exclaims, "Listen! I hear horses."

The second says, "That must be him. All of the other guests of the king are inside."

The first says, "I can hear his horses. It sounds like the servants are taking them to the stables."

The second says, "Stand ready."

Watching through the bushes, the three men see Banquo come into view with Fleance, who carries a torch to light their path.

"That's him," the third whispers to the others.

The first replies, "Stand ready."

Banquo's voice drifts over to them. "It looks like there will be rain tonight."

The first hidden man shouts, "Then let it come down!" as he leaps through the bushes. The other two come through with him, their daggers drawn and ready.

Banquo's eyes widen in shock but quickly narrow as anger overtakes him. He draws his sword. "Oh, the treachery! Fly, Fleance. Fly! I will hold them off."

The boy drops his torch and flees back down the path. The third man moves to catch him, but Banquo strikes at him with his sword, making the other stop for fear that he be impaled on the blade. The other two men move to surround Banqo.

The sky is darkening and the torch light casts flickering long shadows of the four men, and they stand so still only the shadows seem to move. Banquo's eyes move from one man to the next, taking them in. Not a single one has the stance of a fighter. Each holds their knife as if they have hardily had the use of them. In fact, they hold them as one would garden tools. Still, three against one, even sword against knives, he has little hope without armor.

The first man attacks. Banquo steps up to him, catching the small blade with his sword and flinging it aside. The dagger flies out of the man's grasp. Banquo cannot finish his opponent off though, for he needs to turn immediately to the next attacker. He slashes with his sword, cutting the other across his chest. Blood instantly wells up from the wound, but it is not deep enough to even reach muscle.

The first man grabs Banquo's sword arm, wrapping around the muscled limb and pulling his weight on it. Banquo strikes out with his fist at the third, who now attacks. He feels the bone and cartilage in the other's nose pop and break under his assault. Banquo smiles despite himself, seeing the nose is flattened, and blood gushes.

Banquo swings at the man holding his arm, but the other lets go and leaps back. The sword flashes toward his gut. The third man jumps on Banquo from behind, wrapping his arms around the lord's neck and pulling back, putting his weight to work. Banquo's back arches, and his free hand immediately goes to pull on the forearm around his neck. He tries to slash behind himself with the blade but finds it ineffectual at such an angle.

The first man, feeling emboldened, picks up his fallen dagger and rushes the hapless Banquo. He pulls his arm back and stabs down, plunging the dagger deep into Banquo's chest.

"You bastard!" Banquo shouts as his blood flows over the other man's arms and chest. "Flee Fleance and find vengeance."

Banquo's eyes lose focus and his strength gives out. He falls to his knees. His head lulls forward, and his body stills. The three men look at him, one holding his flattened nose, the other pushing a cloth on his bleeding chest. The torchlight goes out.

The flat nosed man says, "Who put out the light?"

The first answers, "Wasn't that for the best? I don't want to draw more attention. Not with you two so bloodied."

The third replies, "But we only got the father."

The second says, "We failed in half of our task.

The first says, "Well, let's get away and tell Macbeth what we did accomplish."

Chapter 4

A large wooden table spans across the dining hall of the Palace of Scone. There are twelve chairs around the table laden with a banquet. Lords and ladies, as well as their numerous attendants, stand at the edge of the room, mingling. Macbeth enters and all conversation stops as they turn to bow to the new king. Lady Macbeth, Ross, and Lennox enter with him.

Macbeth raises his hands and addresses the room. "You know your rank in the peerage. Please sit according to file as I offer you a hearty welcome."

The lords and ladies begin to file to their chairs while their attendants stay by the walls. Macbeth smiles at them, pleased.

"While we eat, I will walk around mingling with you and play the humble host. My wife, your hostess, will keep to her seat but I will have you all welcome her."

Lady Macbeth says, "Do welcome all of your friends for me, sir, for my heart welcomes them all."

"And they reply to you with their thanks." He clasps his hands in delight. "Now that we all have our spots, I will sit among you. Be overburdened in happiness. Soon we will toast."

Servants begin to move into the room carrying sliver trays laden with all manner of food for the feast. They move along the table in a line circling the lords and ladies, depositing splendors when requested. While the serving is done, Macbeth notices one of the men he sent after Banquo appear in the doorway. He casually walks that way while the others are distracted by the food.

Macbeth stands next to the man, leaning against the wall and looking the room over. "There's blood on your face," he states matter-of-factly.

"Then it must be Banquo's. Or maybe my companions. They were injured."

"I must be honest that I rather see his blood on your face than in his veins. Is the deed done then?"

"My lord, he breaths no more. I dispatched him myself."

"Then you are the best of the cutthroats. And whoever removed Fleance would be as good as you. If you did both, then you are a man of unparallel skill."

"Most royal sir, I'm sorry to tell you that Fleance escaped."

The color drains from Macbeth's face, and his breath is caught in his throat. "I must confess I am most disappointed."

"Sorry, my lord. Banquo made it so we could not give chase when the boy ran. When we were done with him, we were not in the shape to give chase."

Macbeth looks down, kicking his hill softly against the wall. "And I can feel my fit again." He clenches his hands into fists. "I thought I was made complete again, solid as marble, firm as rock, free as the air itself. But now…." He seems to fall into himself, compacting under the weight of his sin. "Now I am confined again, all tangled with my doubts and fears." He looks back to the other man. "But Banquo is no longer a threat?"

"Yes, my good lord. He lays dead in a ditch with twenty deep gashes in his chest, and the least of them enough to have ended his life."

"I thank you for that. The adult snake is dead. The young one that escaped has no poison yet, but that threat will grow. You should go now. I will speak with you again tomorrow."

"As you wish." The man bows and departs.

Lady Macbeth addresses the king now that the other has left. "My royal lord, you are not entertaining our guests. If you do not welcome them, they will feel as if they must pay for their meal. It is best to eat at home, but when you eat with others, a little ceremony is expected. The party will be boring without it."

Macbeth smiles to the room warmly. "How kind of you to remind me my duty." He raises his glass in a toast. "Good digestion depends on good appetite, so here is to the health of both."

The party toasts back in general merriment.

Lennox says, "My lord, if it pleases you, please join us at your seat."

"Of course...." Macbeth stops speaking as he watches entering from the far side of the room is Banquo. His eyes do not focus on anything as he makes his way across the room. He steps silently around the table and sits in Macbeth's chair. Banquo's flesh is white as if covered in lye, as are his clothes. Peering closer, the king notices that his old friend is translucent as he can see a hazy image of the lord sitting on the other side of him. Banquo's head turns to Macbeth and locks stares with completely black eyes.

Macbeth forces his voice to come again, hoping nobody saw his fright. "We have all of our country's honored folk under one roof, all but Banquo. I would rather find he is late out of rudeness than that something unspeakable happened to him."

Ross says, "His absence, sir, means he broke his promise to your highness. Why don't you come sit and grace us with your royal company?"

"The table is full," Macbeth replies.

"Here is a place for you, sir," Lennox says, indicating to Macbeth's seat that the phantom of Banquo occupies.

"Where?" Macbeth asks, his eyes not focusing on anything but Banquo.

"Here, my good lord," Lennox answers, again pointing to the chair. "Is something wrong, your heighness?"

His feet rooted to the carpet, Macbeth nearly whispers, "Which of you have done this?"

The lords look among themselves, confused. Ross asks, "What, my good lord?"

Macbeth shouts at the ghost of Banquo, "You cannot say I

did it! Never shake that gory head at me."

Ross says, "Gentlemen, please rise. His highness is not well today."

The lords stand, but Lady Macbeth rises to her feet as well, holding out her hands and prompting the others to sit back down. They do so, reluctantly, some of them looking at her while the others watch her husband. "Sit down, worthy friends. My lord is like this often. It is a malady he has had since childhood. Please remain seated. It only lasts momentarily. He will be well shortly. If you pay too much attention, it will make him angry. Eat and pay him no attention." She walks around the table and stands next to Macbeth, her back to the lords. "Are you a man?"

Macbeth still stares at the ghost while he replies to his wife. "Yes I am, and a bold one at that. I dare stare at what would appall the devil himself!" he growls.

"Oh, that's nonsense! This is just another one of your hallucinations you get from fear. It's like that floating dagger that led you to Duncan. These fits of yours don't even look like real fear but more like a woman's fireside scary story shared with her grandmother. Shame on you! Stop making these faces. When the vision passes, you'll see you are staring at an empty chair."

"But please just look over there. Look! Behold! Can't you see it?" he points to the chair where Banquo sits, staring with his empty, black eyes.

Lady Macbeth turns and sees nothing there.

"What do you have to say now? If the dead are going to return from the grave, then nothing stops the birds from eating the bodies. There would be no point in burying people."

The ghost vanishes from the chair, fading away from Macbeth's vision.

Lady Macbeth snaps, "Has your foolishness paralyzed you?"

"As sure as I'm standing here, I saw Banquo."

"Nonsense!" she barks quietly.

Macbeth says, "Blood has been shed here before in ages past before our laws made the land peaceful. Since then, murders most heinous have been preformed. And it used to be when a man's brains were knocked out, he would die, but now he rises from the dead and walks around, pushing us off of our stools. Haunting is more strange than murder ever was."

Her eyes flutter over the table, taking in all of their guests, who try to not stare at the royal couple. She turns back to the king and whispers in his ear, "My worthy lord, your noble friends miss your company."

Macbeth's eyes widen in surprise. "I do admit I forgot about them." He raises his voice to address the others. "Do not be alarmed, my most worthy friends. I have a strange infirmity, which is nothing to those who know me well." He raises his glass in another toast. "To the love and health of you all. I'll sit with you now. More wine steward. Fill my cup."

The servant pours Macbeth more wine, and he moves to sit at the table. As he takes the first couple steps, the ghost of Banquo reappears in the chair. Macbeth stalls and calls out quite loudly, as if desiring someone from a distance to overhear him, "I drink to the general joy of everyone at the table, and to our dear friend Banquo, whom we miss this evening. How I wish he were here with us! To him and everyone we drink."

"To our duties and the pledge!" the lords echo one another. They all impart a drink from their cups.

Macbeth shouts, "Go, and leave my sight!"

The lords jump in fright at the sudden demand.

"Remain in your grave, hidden from the world. Your bones have no marrow and your body is cold. Though you stare, you do not see anything with those eyes!"

Lady Macbeth addresses the lords before they flee, "My good peers, think of this as but a strange custom. It is nothing more. The only sin in it is the spoiling of our evening pleasure."

"I am as brave as any man. Come at me like a rugged Russian bear, an armed rhinoceros, or an Iranian tiger. Take any shape but the one you now possess and I shall never tremble against you. Or just be alive again and call me out in duel, in a deserted place with swords. If I am afraid then, call me a little girl. But, horrible shadow, unreal mockery of my sanity, flee! Leave here at once."

The ghost of Banquo again vanishes with a wicked looking grin on its transparent face, its deep eyes sparkling with the little light that can escape their depts.

Macbeth sighs in relief and declares, "I am a man again. Look, it is gone. Please, remain seated with me."

Lady Macbeth says quietly to him, "You have ruined our mirth and disrupted the gathering by making a spectacle of yourself."

The king says to the gathering, "Can such things happen, overcoming us like a summer's swift cloud, without leaving us astonished? You make me feel strange, the way you behold these odd sights and keep a straight face while mine has gone white with fear."

Ross dares ask, "What odd sights, my lord?"

Lady Macbeth twirls to Ross. "Please, I ask you don't speak to him. He is only growing worse as the night unfolds. Questions will merely enrage him. Everyone, I do apologize I must ask you to leave for this night. Don't bother standing upon order as you leave, but just go."

"My lady," Lennox says. "I understand. Good night, and I hope for the king's better health."

"A kindly good night to you all!" Lady Macbeth says as they shuffle out of the room, leaving her with Macbeth.

He says to her, "The dead will have their revenge, they say. Blood demands blood. Gravestones have been known to move, and trees speak to bring guilty men to justice. The craftiest murderers have been exposed by mystical signs made by crows and magpies." He looks out the windows. "How late is it?"

Lady Macbeth says, "It is approaching morning already."

"What do you make of it that Macduff would deny me his company?"

"You sent for him?" she asks.

"I heard it from another that he would not come at my call, but I will send for him to see. I fear that every lord has paid spies to watch me from my own servants. Tomorrow, I will go and find the witches. They shall speak to me more. I am determined to know what is going to happen. My safety is the only important thing at the moment. I have waded so far into the blood that it would be just as hard to go back as it would be to continue killing. I have some schemes in my head I would act on but desire their council first."

"You haven't' slept," Lady Macbeth says.

"Then come, and we shall sleep. My self-delusions just come from inexperience. They will pass with time."

Chapter 5

Under the thunder, the tree witches approach three other women standing shoulder to shoulder, backs together, a triangle formed of their bodies. They are covered in robes, hiding everything but their faces. They are middle-aged each with long hair tied back into braids. The one facing forward holds a torch in each hand, though the light does not shine upon anything, instead seeming to cast darkness. The one on the right holds forward a large ring of keys. The one on the left holds a leash attached to a giant wolf dog that sits next to the three.

The first witch says, "Why, my goddess Hecate, do you look so angry?"

"Do I not have reason, disobedient as you are?" the three women say together, one voice higher and another lower, making the three voices sound together to be all encompassing, as if they carry the entirety of existence in a single syllable. "Saucy and overbold, how dare you traffic knowledge to Macbeth in riddles about matters of death. Am I not the source of your powers, the one who decides what deeds happen? And yet you never called upon me in this matter. And what is worse, you have done this for a man who acts like a spoiled brat. Angry and hateful, he chases his desires and has no love for you."

The three witches throw themselves down prostrate before

their goddess's anger. The first proclaims, "I was tricked into it by my sisters. I meant no harm."

The second pushes the first. "Listen not to her, dear Hecate. She always tells us which way we shall walk."

The first says, "It was here, my sister number three. She is the one with the visions, the one who said what we must do."

"The vision was mine," the third confirms, "but I made no mechanization with Macbeth. It was my sisters' plan."

"Silence!" Hecate demands. "I want no excuses. You are to make amends now."

"Oh, please, our goddess," the three say together.

"Go away from this area and meet me in the morning at the pit of Acheron, the river in hell. Macbeth will come to know his destiny. You will take your cauldrons and spells and charms. I'll spend the night fixing this mess of yours, brewing up a fatal end. Great business will be wrought before noon." The three heads look skyward, through the clouds that cover the sky. "Upon the corner of the moon hands a droplet of importance. I'll catch it before it falls and work it by magic to produce spirits that will trick Macbeth with illusions, drawing him into further confusion."

The faces look back to the earth, the front one back to the witches. "He will be fooled into thinking he is greater than fate itself, that he can mock death and live above wisdom, grace, and fear. Overconfidence is the mortals' greatest enemy."

The witches stand again. "As you command us," the first says to Hecate. She looks to her sisters then. "Come and make haste. We must not tarry on her desires."

Chapter 6

Lennox meets with Menteith in the maze of Scone, away from the palace and prying eyes. They work their way deep into the knot of passages until they think nobody could have followed them there deeply without getting lost in the maze.

Lennox says to the other lord, "I think our prior discussion shows we are of like minds. I pray you draw your own conclusions on this as well, but I have seen some strange tidings here. Our gracious King Duncan was pitied by Macbeth after his passing. And valiant Banquo went walking much too late. If you like, we can say Fleance must have killed him and fled, just as the king's sons. Clearly, men should not go walking so late!"

"Or have male children!" the Menteith says.

"And who cannot wonder how monstrous it was for Malcolm and Donalbain to kill their gracious father. Such a heinous crime, and how it did grieve Macbeth as if Duncan was his father as well. Did he not kill those two servants so suddenly while they were in the thralls of drink and sleep? Wasn't that nobly done?"

"Indeed!" the other agrees.

"Yes, and it was the wise thing as well. We would have been so outraged at their denials of their deed. Considering all of this patricide, I think Macbeth has handled things well thus far. If only he had Duncan's sons locked up, which I hope doesn't happen. They would learn how awful the punishment is for killing their father. And so should Fleance."

"Aye."

"But enough for such words. I hear Macduff is out of the king's favor as well because he speaks too plainly and failed to show up to Macbeth's feast. Can you tell me where he is hiding?"

Menteith answers, "As you know, Duncan's son Malcolm, who's birthright and throne Macbeth has stolen, lives in the English court. The pious Edward welcomes him well despite Malcolm's misfortune, treating him with the respect one of his station deserves. Macduff went there as well to ask King Edward for help. He wants to seek an alliance formed with the people of Northumberland and Siward. Macduff hopes that with their help— and that of God above—he may once again put food upon our tables and bring peace back to our homes. He wishes for us to be able to pay proper homage to our king and receive honors freely without fear. It is all the things we pine for now. Macbeth knows this and his rage has him preparing for war."

Lennox asks, "So the king sent for Macduff to return?"

"He did, but the reply came back that he would not come. The messenger told him he would regret that was his answer."

Lennox says, "And that may just advise him to keep his distance. Some holy angel should go to the English court and give him a message. Return quickly to free our country suffering under a tyrant."

The lord says, "I will send my prayers with our messenger angel."

Book 4

Chapter 1

Along the Scottish coast is a cave in the bluffs normally hidden underwater. During times of low tide, as it is now, it stands open to the air. Lights flicker over the water formed walls, fighting against lightning flashes for dominance. The flickering comes from a fire that eats driftwood lying in the middle of the open space. The boughs are stacked in a pile and pop and hiss under the heat. The yellow flames lick over the bottom of a cauldron full to the brim with a boiling amalgam of putrid smelling liquids.

The three witches dance and sway around the cauldron, drawn into rapture revealed by their moans and squeals of delight.

The first calls out, "The orange cat has meowed thrice!"

The second follows, "Three times! And the hedgehog whined once."

The third says, "Harpier, my spirit friend, an owl of great presence, calls out! 'It's time, it's time!' he says."

"Round the cauldron we go, dancing. And into the potion we throw poisoned entrails." The first witch holds up a toad over the boiling putrid mass. "A toad, from under a cold rock for a month, sweltering venom. I will boil you first in the charmed pot!" She drops the toad in. It does not sink right through the surface, but plops on top of the thick, rolling mass. The toad's legs kick as it twitches in its death throes, cooked from the heat while alive, and its body dissolves where it touches the cauldron's contents.

The three hags call out together, "Double, double toil and trouble, fire burn, and cauldron bubble."

"We'll boil and bake you in the cauldron next. In with the snake!" The second witch drops a cobra into the pot, finding its fate the same as the now disappeared toad. As she throws in more ingredients, she calls them out in turn. "Eye of newt and toe of frog, wool of bat and tongue of dog. Adder's fork and stinger of a burrowing worm. A lizard's leg and owlet's wing. All for a charm to cause powerful trouble, like a broth from hell. Boil and bubble."

Again the three call out together, "Double, double toil and trouble, fire burn and cauldron bubble."

The third begins throwing in more ingredients. "Scale of a dragon, tooth of a wolf. The mummified flesh of a witch, stomach and jaws of a hungry shark, root of hemlock found in the dark. The liver of a blaspheming Jew, a goat's bile, twigs and yew broken from under the moon's eclipse. The nose of a Turk, and a Tartar's lips. Finger of a baby birthed of a prostitute in a ditch and strangled with its own cord. It will make the gruel thick and gluey." She says to her sisters, "Now we need the tiger's entrails."

"Double, double toil and trouble, fire burn and cauldron bubble," they call out again.

The first drops in the tiger's guts.

Then, the second calls out, "And finally, we cool it with the blood of a baboon." The pot hisses as it cools with the blood pouring into it. "The charm is strong and well made. It will do evil most heinous."

"Well done!" a symphony of three female voices boom out. Standing by the cave walls is Hecate with her wolf-dog. "I commend your pains, and each of you will share in the rewards. Now sing around the cauldron like the elves and fairies of old, enchanting the mixture as you spin."

The witches twirl around and around the cauldron again, singing out loud as commanded. As they move, Hecate vanishes, leaving the witches alone.

They dance as such for half an hour before the second stops suddenly and says, "By the tingling of my thumbs, I can feel something wicked coming this way. Open the door for whoever knocks."

All three of the witches look to the cave's opening, where Macbeth is walking toward them, looking annoyed as he brushes at his damp and torn dirty clothes. He steps up to the witches and demands, "What are you doing here, you hags of secret and evil things that stalk the night?"

All three call out, "A deed without a name."

"Whatever," Macbeth says, dismissing the answer with a wave of his hand. "I don't know where you learned the things you told me, but I want answers now. And I don't care for you threats. Go ahead and call down winds to tear churches apart, to make the ocean's currents spin about ships and swallow them whole. Go ahead and blow down trees and our crops and make castles fall upon their inhabitants' heads. Collapse palaces and pyramids, and mix up the wonders of nature if you wish. But you will tell me what I need to know."

The first says, "Speak."

The second replies, "Demand."

The third says, "We'll answer."

The first steps away from the cauldron and up to Macbeth, making him wince and take a step back from her smell. When she speaks, he steps back a second time from her breath. "Would you rather hear the answers from our mouths, or from our masters'?"

"Call them. I would look upon your dark masters. I am not afraid."

"So be it," the first says. She turns back to her sisters and points to the cauldron. "Pour in a sow's blood who has eaten her nine piglets. Take the sweat of a murderer in the gallows and throw it into the fire."

The other two do as the first asks. The three call out after, "Come spirits of both high and low. Show yourself and what you do."

Thunder booms out as an apparition appears. It is merely a giant head, floating without a body in the cave. A helmet sits upon its brow with a mane of horse hair like the Spartans of old. Its eyes

80

are merely empty sockets with dried blood that had run down onto its cheeks. Its mouth is gaping open with no teeth and a swollen tongue.

Macbeth stares at the monstrous sight and finds his limbs seized with terror, but the frightful visage does not keep him from speaking. "I beseech you, tell me, you unknown power...."

The first witch warns the king, "He knows your thoughts. Listen to his words but do not speak."

The apparition says, "Macbeth! Macbeth! Macbeth!" Despite its swollen tongue, its voice comes out in a harsh whisper, clearly audible. "Beware Macduff. Beware the Thane of Fife. Let me go, witches. Enough." The head fades and sinks into the floor.

"Whatever you are, I thank you for your advice," Macbeth calls to the spirit. "You have spoken my fears to me, but I want one more word."

The first witch steps forward with a raised arm, pointing a crocked finger toward him. "He will not be commanded by you and your ilk. But I will call another, more potent than the first."

A bloody hand rises out of the ground, grabbing a rock that is solid to it whereas the rest of the ground is not. The hand is small, less than half the size of Macbeth's. A child's hand, he realizes. A second arm rises, and it lifts itself up. Its wispy haired head rises up, pulling its body into view. It stands on bowed legs, a naked and bloody child of less than two years.

It shouts out in a whispering voice that sounds more like air is sucked into its small body than exhaled. "Macbeth! Macbeth! Macbeth!"

"If I had three ears, I'd listen with all three," the king answers.

The bloody babe calls out, "Be bloody, and bold, and do not waiver. Laugh to ridicule the powers of other men, because nobody born of a woman shall harm Macbeth." The apparition fades and passes back into the ground.

"Then let Macduff live. What fear should I hold for him?" Macbeth says in elation. "But still, I'll make doubly sure and guarantee my fate. I'll still kill him and in such conquer my fear and find sleep once again."

A third apparition fades into view before the cauldron, unbidden. It looks as a child like the last, but his one is not covered in blood. It instead wears a crown upon its head.

Macbeth asks, "What is this spirit that looks like the son of a king and wears a crown upon its brow?"

All three witches shout at Macbeth, "Listen but do not speak to it!"

The spirit talks, and its voice is booming, sounding like that of a giant of a grown man, but its mouth does not move with the voice. "Be brave like a lion, proud, and worry not about those who hate and resent you or conspire against you. Macbeth shall never be vanquished until the Great Birnam Woods marches to fight you on Dunsinane Hill." The spirit then vanishes as quickly as it came.

"Then I shall rejoice!" Macbeth beams. "That will never happen. Who can make the forest move, to command trees to pull up their roots and march on me? These are sweet omens! Good! Then I shall be king for the rest of my natural life. I thank you three witches for these favors, but I must ask one more thing. Banquo's sons. Will they ever rise to reign over this kingdom?"

The three witches call out together in one voice, warning, "Seek no more knowledge."

"I will be satisfied," Macbeth demands. "If you deny me this, then let an eternal curse fall upon you! Answer me. I command you to do so."

The cauldron begins to sink into the stone, passing through the burning wood, leaving the fire and timbers it consumes untouched. Confused and frightened, Macbeth asks, "Why is your cauldron sinking into the stone?"

The first witch cries out, "Show."

The second does the same, and finally the third calls, "Show."

Their voices rise up in unison once more. "Show him and let his heart grieve. Come like shadows and depart in the same."

Shades of men march out of the cavern wall. Each wears a crown and is covered by a royal cape. The kings march across

Macbeth's view. He flinches at each of them as if finding pain in their mere existence. The first in line is not dressed as a king like the rest, but it is instead the ghost of Banquo's itself, looking just as it did at the feast in the Palace of Scone.

"Your crown hurts my eyes!" he shouts to the first following Banquo. Macbeth tries to divert his attention to the second but finds it even more painful. "Your golden hair shines like another crown beneath the one you wear." He looks back to the first. "You look the same!" he exclaims.

The third, he sees, also appears similar to the other two. He cries out to the witches, "Filthy hags! Why do you show me this?" Macbeth screams in fright as a forth walks out of the cavern wall. "No more." He sees a fifth, finding its eyes protruding out of the skull as if kiwi fruit too large to fit into the sockets. "Will this line stretch out to the end of time? And another? A seventh?" he shouts as two more march past. An eighth comes out of the wall, carrying a hand mirror. In the deepness of the reflection, Macbeth sees a long line of kings stretching out many times more than these mere eight.

"Those in the mirror," Macbeth says in horror. "Some are carrying double and triple scepters. They are king of more than one country. What a horrible sight! Now I see it is true. They are Banquo's descendants. They have his golden hair. They look just like him. Fleance then made good his escape."

The progression of kings vanishes into another wall with the ghost of Banquo leading them. Macbeth turns back to the witches then. "Is this so?"

The first witch cackles. "Aye, sir, it is so. But why do you stand there so dumbfounded? We already foretold those events. Come, sisters, let's cheer him up with our best delights. I'll charm the air to perform music while we dance so this king will say we did our duty to entertain him. We must stand on duty after all."

Music begins to pay from the very air, and the witches twirl once more in dance. Quickly, their forms begin to fade until they too disappear much like the spirits. And with the cauldron completely vanished into the floor, there is nothing remaining save the fire.

"Have they truly gone? Were they ever really here?" Macbeth asks himself out loud. "Let this evil hour be ever marked as cursed." He turns to the mouth of the cave and shouts, "You there. Outside. Come in!"

The nobleman Lennox enters the cave, looking around cautiously. "What is your grace's will?"

"Did you see the witches?"

"No, my lord," Lennox answers. "Witches?"

"Did they not pass you?"

"Indeed not, my lord. Are you feeling well?" Lennox asks.

"The air upon which they ride is infected with evil. Damned are all of those who trust their words!"

"My lord, if it pleases you, I received a message while I waited for you to complete your business here, whatever that was."

"Speak then," Macbeth commands.

"Macduff has fled to England."

"To England?"

"Yes, my good lord."

"Time always thwarts my dreadful plans. Unless I act upon them the second the idea comes to me, I'll never get the chance to go through with it. From now on, as soon as I make a decision, I will act upon it immediately. In fact, I'll start now by raiding Macduff's castle and seizing the town of Fife."

"My lord?" Lennox asks, uncertain if he heard right.

"I will kill his wife, his children, and all of the unfortunate souls that stand in line for his inheritance. No more boasting like a fool. I will do this deed before my thoughts cool and I lose my nerve. Come. We have work to do."

Chapter 2

Unlike the eloquent Palace at Scone, Macduff's castle was not only constructed from bricks and mortar, but that was also the finishing materials as well. No wooden beams cross ceilings, no carpets span the floors, and only small glass windows let sunlight in. The artwork is sparse and the furniture plain. The castle falls short of the wealth of Macduff, but he preferred to keep it as such. Frugal Macduff would not spend the wealth to remodel the castle as it would help nothing but his pride, and no satisfaction can be found in pride.

In a meeting hall of the castle, Lady Macduff talks with Ross, while her young son stands near the door, listening.

"What did that husband of mine do to make him want to flee Scotland?" the lady demands.

"You must have patience, madam," Ross says.

"Why? He had none. It was madness to run as he did. Even if you are not a traitor, running makes you look guilty. He should have learned that lesson from Duncan's sons."

"Please, my lady, you cannot know whether it was in wisdom or fear that he fled."

"Wisdom! How could it be wisdom, to leave his wife and children, his home and titles in a place so unsafe that he flees it? He does not love us. Even the smallest bird, the wren, will fight when her young are threatened by an owl. He ran from his fear, not for love. It is unreasonable for him to run, so it could not have been wisdom."

Ross sighs. He takes a second to gather his thoughts before speaking to the difficult woman. "My dearest cousin, I beg you to pull yourself together. Your husband is noble, wise, and judicious. He knows what is best for the problems we face. I can't say more though. We live in times where people are being denounced as traitors and don't know why. We believe in frightful rumors in such times but don't even know what we are actually afraid of. It's like being thrown around by the violent sea and getting nowhere."

She glares at him, understanding what he says but still not believing.

Ross steps up to her and grabs her hand. "I must take my leave, but I shall not be long before returning." He pulls her forward and whispers into her ear, "When things are at their worst, they must stop, or at least return to where they were before. My pretty cousin, I give you my blessings."

Lady Macduff pulls away and looks upon Ross with hard and angry eyes. She tilts her head, indicating her son. "He has a father, and yet he's fatherless. Do you not understand? My husband has failed us in doing what he thinks is right."

"What I understand is this. Danger is coming for us all. If you will take my simple advice, you will flee from here, otherwise they will know where to find you. Go, and take the child with you. I feel bad to frighten you like this, but it would be much worse if you do not flee. I bring you this warning as a friend to Macduff, and as your cousin. May God keep you and your children safe."

"And where should I go, Ross? I have done nothing wrong. Why should I run? But I remember that I'm on this world, where doing evil is often admired, and doing good is sometimes a dangerous mistake."

"And doing nothing can be the worst sin of all," Ross replies. "I would be a fool to stay any longer, as would you." He steps back and looks at her for a few awkward seconds. He turns his back to her and says, "Should I stay longer? I will disgrace myself and embarrass you with my tears. I must leave at once. Stay strong, for your family."

Ross courtly leaves from her sight, and she knows he flees the castle shortly after as she watches him through a window riding his horse away. She should leave as well, but it is so difficult to flee from one's home. Safety for herself and her child is paramount though, even though her husband fled and left them to face the danger alone. How could that be anything but an act of cowardice? Responsibility to one's family is the first duty, before that to country. Is it not, she wonders?

Lady Macduff looks over to her son and calls him over. She sits down and pats her lap. He climbs up with her help to sit across her legs. She flattens his hair with her hand, fixing a few rebellious strands. Though her husband forgot the first duty, she had not.

"Young man, your father's dead. What will you do now? How will you live?"

"As the birds do, mother," he replies without hesitation.

"I don't understand. Will you live off of worms and flies?"

"What I mean to say, is that I will get by with whatever I can get."

"You would make such a pitiful bird. You wouldn't know enough to avoid pitfalls," Lady Macduff says.

"Why should I, mother? If I'm such a pitiful bird, then hunters will not want me. Besides, despite what you are saying, I know my father is not dead."

Lady Macduff smirks at him. "And yet, he is dead. What will you do for a father?"

"Maybe you should ask what you will do for a husband."

She fully smiles now. "Why, I can buy myself twenty of those at any market."

"Then you will only be buying them to sell them back."

"My son, you talk like a child, but you have great wit. Where do you learn such things?"

"Was my father a traitor, mother?"

"Yes, that he was," Lady Macduff says.

"What is a traitor?" he asks.

"It's someone who makes a promise and breaks it."

"Is everyone who swears an oath and breaks it a traitor?" the boy asks.

"Every one of them, and they must be hanged."

"So everyone who makes promises and breaks them need to be hung?"

"Every one," Lady Macduff acknowledges.

"Who must hang them?"

"Only an honest man can."

"Then the liars and oath breakers are fools."

"Oh?"

"Yes," he says in all seriousness. "There are many more of them than honest men, so the liars should get together and hang the honest men."

Lady Macduff stares at him for a second in horror, thinking that maybe that is exactly what is happening. Her face softens then as she begins to roar with laughter. "Now, God help you, my poor boy!" He fixes him in a stare. "But you still haven't answered my question. What will you do for a father?"

"I don't need to do anything. If my father was dead, you would be weeping for him. If he is dead and you are not weeping, then that is a good sign I will quickly have a new father."

"Where do you hear of these things!" she exclaims. "It didn't come from me."

She puts her son back down and stands up. Looking back down upon him, she quietly asks herself, "Why do I put up this womanly defense that I am innocent of wrongs? My coward husband's problems are now our problems."

"My lady?" a servant calls with a wavering voice dripping with fear.

Lady Macduff looks to the doorway and sees one of her retainers standing there. The woman has a concerned look across her face. It is obvious as to why, for three men stand around her, one on each side and one behind her. Each carries a knife in their hands.

Shaking, Lady Macduff says, "That will be all," dismissing the attendant.

The men move aside for the woman to depart. She all but runs down the hallway to escape. The three step into the room and regard Lady Macduff.

"Who are you three?" she demands, letting her outrage at being disturbed unbidden keep the shaking from her voice.

The first man asks, "Where is your husband?"

She flinches at the question. "I hope not in a place so scandalous that ruffians like you can find him."

The first man barks out a short laugh. "He's a traitor. Everywhere he goes is made scandalous for his very presence."

The lady's son stomps forward a step and says with his strongest voice, "You lie, you shaggy haired villain!"

The man blinks quickly as if slapped in the face. "What's that, you runt?"

The assassin charges forward. Lady Macduff first shies away but sees the man moves toward her son instead of herself. She steps forward to meet the man and protect her child. He backhands her so hard the world begins to spin. She falls to the floor, her eyes downcast as she holds the side of her head.

"You son of a traitor!" the man hollers.

Lady Macduff looks back up just as the tip of the knife blade pierces her son's abdomen, plunging deeply into his soft gut. His hips are pushed back quickly, but his shoulders and arms stay forward, making him bend nearly in half, appearing as if he is held up merely by the dagger. The murderer pulls up on the blade, slicing upward through the soft muscle wall, and the son of Macduff's insides spill out onto the floor. He grabs for his intestines, holding them as one would a prized possession as he falls to his rump.

He looks to his mother, his eyes wide open in surprise, but his mouth is twisted in rage. "I'm dead, mother. But you can still flee."

"But...," she tries to speak but he cuts her off.

"Run!" he yells, making more of his insides flop out under the strain. "I beg you. Run." His small body falls backward. His hands still move, holding his intestines, trying to put them back inside the wound, but his movements are small and weak as little strength remains.

Crying hysterically at seeing her son disemboweled, she gains her feet with strength she did not think she still possessed. She runs, crying out, "Murder!" hoping that the guards will come.

"Don't let her get away!" the first assassin says to the other two. They give chase as the first one turns back to the boy to make sure the job is done.

The guards do not come in time.

Chapter 3

"I'm so pleased to see you, my old friend. Come, let's find some shady place where we can weep our sad hearts out," Malcolm says to Macduff as soon as they were alone.

Macduff had arrived earlier this day, hoping to do so silently to more easily perform his deed and be on his way, but that was not to be. As soon as he arrived, everyone was standing on presentation, greeting the Scottish lord. He cursed his luck silently while showing gratitude to the English court. It took most of the day before he could get Malcolm away from the crowds.

Macduff says to his prince, "Instead of crying, I would rather hold fast to our swords like the honorable men we are and defend our homeland. Every morning, there are more women finding out there are widows, as are there more children discovering they are now orphans. New sorrows strike Scotland in the face until it sounds like the whole of the country is filled with anguished screams."

Malcolm looks at the other with a penetrating eye, realizing the appearance of the other is not such a fanciful visit as he first thought. "I will speak for only what I believe in. And I believe only what I am certain is the truth. What you have said is perhaps true. The tyrant's very name hurts to speak, but he was once considered an honest man like so many others."

Macduff opens his mouth to speak, but Malcolm raises a

hand to still him.

"You used to love him yourself, and you have not yet been harmed. I am young still, but I see that you may be trying to betray me to him, and in such win his favor. It would be smart to offer up a weak and poor innocent lamb like me to appease such an angry god. A sacrifice to the lord of a volcano."

Macduff looks at the other in surprise. "I am not here out of treachery."

"But Macbeth is treacherous himself. A good and virtuous man may be tempted by a royal charge, as duty commands." Malcolm's eyes drop down. "But I do beg your pardon. My fears cannot make you into a dishonest man. Angels will remain bright even though Lucifer, who was the brightest among them, fell to his own deceitfulness. Even the foulest soul will want to appear as one with grace, and it often succeeds. But goodness still has to look fair, or it will be mistaken as evil."

Macduff looks downtrodden. His eyes break from the prince's gaze. "I have lost my hopes for this visit. I thought you a better man than to leave you countrymen unprotected."

"Maybe you lost your hope pertaining to me, but I found doubts in you. Why did you leave your wife and child? Aren't they the things most precious to you?"

"How dar…."

Malcolm raises a hand to still the other. "Don't let my suspicions insult you. You must understand it is for my own safety. You might be being honest with me, whatever it is I may think."

Macduff begins marching back and forth, throwing his arms up in frustration. "Our country is bleeding to death! Macbeth builds himself up as a great tyrant. And it is the goodness in people that makes them dare not stand up to you. Enjoy what it is you stole as your title is safe as we don't have the heart to take it away." He stops and looks back to the prince. "Farewell, lord. I would not be the scoundrel you believe me capable of being even if I was offered the whole of Scotland and the riches of the east."

"Do not be offended. I do not speak in complete distrust of you. I understand Scotland is sinking under the tyrant's rule. It weeps and bleeds for each new wound added to her, wounds that come hourly. I think there are many who would fight for me back home, and many thousands of soldiers have been promised from gracious England as well. But despite all of this, when the tyrant's head is under my foot or stuck at the end of my sword, an even greater evil will be upon our poor land. It will suffer further in many more ways under the king who will follow Macbeth."

Macduff is stilled, now thinking there may be more to this than a spoiled boy prince. "Who are you talking about?"

"I mean me, of course. I have so many vices of such strength that when the people see them, evil Macbeth will seem as pure as white snow. Scotland will call him an innocent lamb when compared to my countless evils."

"What?" Macduff scoffs. "Not in the legions of hell could you find a devil worse than Macbeth."

"I freely admit he is a murderous, lecherous, greedy, lying, deceitful, violent, malicious, and guilty of every sin that has a name, and many that don't. But as for me, my sexual desires have no bottom. Your wives, daughters, matrons, and maids could not fill the cup of my lust. My desire would overbear all restraints and anyone who dared to oppose my will. It is better to have one like Macbeth rule than one like me."

"Boundless gluttony in a man's lust is a type of tyranny. It has been cause of many fallen kings. But do not let your fear of this stop you from taking what is yours. You can satisfy your pleasures in abundance while keeping it secret. You can hoodwink everyone in this regard. There are more than enough willing women around. There cannot be so much lust in you to be able to use up all the women willing to give themselves to the king once they find he is so inclined."

"That may be, but along with my lust is my incredible greed. If I were to be king, I would steal the land from the nobles, taking their jewels and houses. And the more I have, the more I will desire, until I would cause quarrels that are undeserved against good and loyal men, destroying them for my desire of wealth. Would you be such a man?"

Macduff rolls his eyes, a habit most unbecoming of a thane. "This greed is deeper and more dangerous than your lust, and it has gotten kings assassinated before. But do not fear. Scotland has many treasures to fill your royal coffers, surely enough to gain you some satisfaction. These negatives are bearable when weighed against your good graces."

Malcolm's voice rises. "Good graces? But I have none. I do not possess any of the good qualities a king needs, as justice, truth, self-control, stability, generosity, perseverance, mercy, humility, devotion, patience, courage, and fortitude. I have no desire of them but am full of desire of so many vices that I act upon. No, if I had power, I would pour the sweet milk of harmony into hell itself, destroy the universal peace, and bewilder all harmony on the planet."

Macduff throws up his hands in disgust. "Oh Scotland, Scotland!" he exclaims.

"If a person such as I would be fit to govern, then speak up. I am exactly as I described to you."

"Fit to be king? You aren't even fit to live." Macduff places his hands on his head in exasperation and walks a few paces away, looking away from the prince. "Oh miserable Scotland, ruled by a usurping tyrant seeped in blood, when shall we see peaceful days again? The only man who has right to the throne is, by his own admission, a cursed man who disgraces his family." He turns back to Malcolm and stalks towards him. "Your royal father was a virtuous king. Your mother spent more time in prayer on her knees than she did standing. She lived a life of complete piety." Macduff throws up his hand and begins to walk away. "Farewell! The evils you share with me have driven me out of Scotland forever. I came for you and cannot go back without you. My hope dies at your lecherous feet!"

Malcolm smiles a devious grin at the older man. "Good Macduff, your passionate outburst has proved to me you are a man of integrity. It removed my doubts about you, answering my worries that you are not a trustworthy and honorable man."

Macduff pauses and turns back to the prince, looking confused.

94

"Macbeth has tried many times to lure me to him, and prudence has kept me alive. But God above as my witness, I will put myself into your council and take back my confessions made to you just now. None of those flaws are a part of my nature. I am still a virgin. I have not spoken a lie to deceive a man save those I just spoke to you. I barely desire what is my own, let alone coveting what another owns. I have never broken a promise, and would not to even the devil himself. I love truth as much as life itself."

"You just lied to me," Macduff says, wary.

"The lies I spoke about myself were the first I have ever spoken. The person who I truly am is ready to serve you and our poor country. Indeed, before you even arrived, old Siward has ten thousand soldiers making way to us here for my use. Now, you will go with me to fight Macbeth, and the chance of our success is must greater for it!" The prince notices Macduff still considers him with disbelieving eyes. "Why are you silent?"

"It's hard to settle such good news and bad news at once. I need to figure out which is true."

Another man approaches them in the courtyard. Malcolm takes notice of him and says to Macduff, "Well, we'll speak more on this soon." He steps towards the newcomer and calls out, "Is King Edward coming out?"

The other says, "Yes, sir. There is a crowd of sick souls that require his healing. Their malady is greater than even our modern medicine can cure. But his touch, by the powers granted from heaven, he can amend their ills."

Malcolm replies, "Thank you, doctor."

The other bows and departs.

Macduff asks, "What disease does he mean?

"It's called the evil. Edward's healing touch is miraculous. I have seen him work it many times since I have been in England. Nobody knows how he asked Heaven for this blessing, but those he uses it on are cured as surely as if they were never sick. They were swollen and ulcerous, pitiful to look upon. They are beyond the help of surgery, but he cures them by placing a golden coin on a chain around their necks and says holy prayers over them. It is said that he will pass this down to his royal descendants. With this strange virtue, he has been given the gift of prophecy as well, among other strange and wonderful abilities. All of these mark him a man in the full grace of God."

"Good sir!" a man yells out to them.

Macduff looks to the approaching man. "Who's that coming to us?"

"He is our countryman by the looks of him, but I do not know him," Malcolm answers.

"My noble kinsman," Macduff calls out, "you are most welcome to join us."

The prince says, "I know him now. May God remove the machinations that keep us apart!"

"Hello, sir," the nobleman greets the other two when he stands among them.

"Good Ross." Macduff greets him with a firm handshake. "Has anything changed since I left?"

"Alas, our poor country!" Ross exasperates. "I'm almost too frightened to know myself. Scotland is no longer the land where we were born, but the land where we will die. It is a land where no one smiles but those who know nothing of the tragedies happening around us. A land where sighs and groans and shrieks rip through the air and are ignored as they are so common now. Sorrow fills everyone full. The funeral bells ring, and nobody asks who has died, for good men die before the flowers in the fields can wilt. They die before they even sicken."

"Your relation is too poetic and all too true." Macduff says

Malcolm asks, "What is the news of Scotland?"

Ross shakes his head in despair. "News from an hour ago is old news as every minute finds another more dreadful thing has happened."

Impatiently, Macduff asks, "How is my wife?"

Ross answers quickly, "Well."

"And my children."

He pauses slightly before saying, "The same."

"The Tyrant has left then be?"

Ross answers, "They were at peace when I left them."

Macduff relaxes slightly at that news. "Now don't be stingy with your words. What brings you here?"

"I came here to pass on sad news, but I heard rumor of many good men arming themselves against the tyrant. I also saw Macbeth's army on the move, and I knew the rumor had to be true. So now is the time when we need your help. Your very presence would inspire both men and women to fight to rid themselves of the tyrant."

Malcolm grasps Ross's shoulder. "Then let them find comfort. We are returning to Scotland. Gracious Edward has lent us Siward and ten thousand men. There is no better or experienced soldier in the entire Christian world."

Ross frowns. "If only I could answer this comfort with happy news of my own. But I have news that should be kept in a barren land where nobody can hear it."

Macduff again feels concern overtake him. "What is this new concern? Is it a general affliction, or is it for just one of us?"

"No honest man can keep from sharing in the same woe, but it pertains to you alone."

Macduff says, "If it is for me, then have at it. Let me hear it quickly. Do not tarry in the telling."

Ross cannot return Macduff's poignant gaze. "I hope you not hate me forever after telling you this, because I must give you the most dreadful news you have ever heard."

Macduff's face ashens. "I can guess at what you are about to say."

"You castle was sacked. Your wife and children were savagely slaughtered. If I were to tell you the manner, it would cause so much pain as to kill you as well and add your death on top of theirs."

"Merciful heaven!" Malcolm yells. "Come on, man! Do not hide your grief. Put words to your sorrow. The grief you keep inside will whisper to your heart and bid it to break."

His voice cracking in pain, Macduff asks, "My children, too?"

Ross says quietly, "Wife, children, servants. Anyone they

could find. Dead."

Tears begin to stream down Macduff's cheeks. "And I had to be away!" He grabs Ross in both hands, holding on to his shoulders for just as much support for his weakened legs as to make the other speak directly to him. "My wife was killed too?"

"As I said. Yes."

Macduff drops his grip and falls to his knees. His face is slacken, his jaw dangling. Tears continue to march down his face.

Malcolm comes up from behind him but does not reach forth to touch the other man. "Take what little comfort I can offer. Let's make a medicine out of our revenge and cure your grief with Macbeth's corpse."

Macduff whispers something nobody else hears.

"What?" Malcolm asks quietly.

"He has no children," he says louder this time. "All my pretty ones? Did you say all? Oh, that man from hell! All? All my pretty children and their mother dead in one fell swoop?"

Malcolm growls in anger, standing just behind the other. "Fight it like a man."

"Oh, I shall do so," he barks out, but in a softer voice says, "But I must also feel it as a man. I cannot help but remember all the little things that were precious to me. Did heaven watch the slaughter and send no help? Sinful Macduff, they were killed because of you! Wicked as I am, it was not for their sins, but for mine. May God grant their souls rest."

Malcolm says, "Let this be the whetstone on which you sharpen your sword. Change that grief into anger. Don't block your heart, but let it enrage."

"I could weep like a woman and brag on how I will avenge them! But gentle heavens, don't keep me waiting. Bring Macbeth to me, face to face, so I can run this fiend through with my own sword, ridding myself and Scotland of him! Put him in reach of my sword, and if he escapes, then may heaven forgive him as well."

Malcolm smiles in finality. "Now you sing the tune of a man. Come. Let us not wait longer. We must speak with King Edward. Our army is ready. All we must do is take our leave. Macbeth is ripe for the picking, and the agents of God have blessed us. Take what joy you can. The long night is finally ending. Day comes."

Book 5

Chapter 1

The sun has set over the palace of Scone hours ago, and a doctor waits with a servant of the king and queen. He is here at the king's orders.

The doctor says to the lady, "I have spent two nights watching with you, but I have not seen what you were talking about. When was the last time you saw her sleepwalking?"

The servant, slightly angry as this turn of events, replies, "It was since his majesty went out to war. I have seen her rise from bed and throw on her nightgown. She unlocks her closet, take out some paper and folds it before writing upon it. She reads it back, seals it, and returns to bed. All the while she is sleeping."

"It is unnatural to act as you are awake while sleeping. When she is like this, have you heard her saying anything? It may give us an idea why this happens."

"Yes she does, sir, but I will not tell you what she says."

"You have to tell me. It could be really important."

The servant looks resolute. "I will not tell you. I will not tell anybody else for that matter, because there was nobody else there to confirm what I heard her say. I don't want to be accused of making rumors."

A noise draws her attention. They both look to the disturbance and find Lady Macbeth walking into the far end of the chamber, holding a candle to light her way.

"Look, here she comes," the servant says, excitement betrayed in her voice. They both kneel down to stay out of sight. "This is exactly how she normally appears. And I swear upon my life that she is asleep. Watch her but keep hidden. You mustn't wake the sleepwalkers. It can be dangerous"

"Where did she find that candle?"

"It is from her bedside. She always has to have a light when she sleeps. Those are her orders."

"Her eyes are open," the doctor says. "Are you sure she is sleeping?"

"Yes, they are open, but they don't see anything."

"What is she doing now?" the doctor asks. "Look how she rubs her hands."

Lady Macbeth indeed is rubbing her hands together, holding them before her as if in a basin. She scrubs furiously at her flesh.

The servant says, "It is an action she does often. It looks like she is washing her hands, and I've seen her do this for as long as fifteen minutes."

Lady Macbeth's voice cries out in frustration. "And there's another spot! Why is it so hard to clean off?"

"Listen!" the doctor utters. "She speaks. I will write down what she says to help me better remember each remark." He pulls out a pad of paper and begins to write all that he hears.

"Come out, damned spot! Out, I say! One, two. It is time to do it."

She turns quickly, no longer scrubbing her hands but still holding them together. "Hell is murky! Nonsense, my lord, nonsense. You are a revered soldier, and yet you are frightened? What fear do we need to feel when no one knows our misdeeds? Nobody can call us out." She turns back and starts working over her hands again furiously. "Yet who would have thought such an old man would be filled with so much blood?"

The doctor's face pales. "Did you hear that?" His hand stops writing, uncertain if such a record would be wise to create.

"The Thane of Fife had a wife. Where is she now?" Lady Macbeth asks. Her head drops back to her hands, seeing with unseeing eyes. "What? Will these hands of mine never be clean? But no more of that, my lord. No more. Enough has been done with such deeds." She again turns away from the basin only she can see. "You will ruin everything by acting in such a fright."

The doctor places the paper down and lets his head droop down. "Now look what you've done. You know that which you should not."

The maid says, "She is saying things that she should not say, I'm sure. Heaven only knows what secrets she knows."

"I can still smell the blood!" Lady Macbeth wrinkles her nose as she sniffs the back of her hand. "All of the perfumes of Arabia could not make this little hand of mine smell better. Oh, oh, oh!"

"What a heavy sigh. Her heart carries a weight I cannot imagine."

The maid, not able to remove her eyes from the queen, says, "I would not wish for such a heart for myself even if it meant making me the queen."

"Well, well, well," the doctor says out of habit when he does not know what to say.

"I pray to God that what she says is well, sir," the maid says.

"I'm afraid this disease is beyond my skills to treat. I have known those who have walked in their sleep and have not been guilty of anything. But for one such as she…."

"Wash your hands! Put on your nightgown. Do not look so frightened. I will tell you yet again that Banquo's buried and cannot come back from his grave."

The doctor addresses the maid, "Is this the truth?"

The maid finds she cannot answer but instead feels her strength waning.

"To bed, to bed. There's someone knocking at the gate," the queen says. "Come, come, come, come. Give me your hand. What we have done cannot be taken back. To bed, to bed, to bed!" She walks off, scrubbing her hands some more, muttering inaudibly now.

"Will she go to bed now?" the doctor asks.

"She will, immediately."

"Rumors of evil are going around. Unnatural acts are causing unnatural troubles. Guilty people confess their sins into pillows as they sleep."

"What can we do for her, doctor?" the maid asks.

"Do for her? She is beyond the help I can provide. She needs God, not a doctor." He looks upward. "God, please forgive us all!" The doctor locks a stare with the maid. "Look after her. Remove anything she might hurt herself or others with. But above all else, do not stop watching her." He stands back up. "And now I must wish you a good night. She has bewitched my mind and amazed my eyes. I have thoughts about what has happened to our queen, but I do not dare speak those words out loud."

"Then good night, doctor. Thank you for coming."

Chapter 2

Lord Lennox rides his horse across a grassy field with Angus next to him. The noblemen Menteith and Caithness follow behind. The four could not be confused with others who may just be out for a casual ride as they are burdened in armor and carry holstered swords. To take away any doubt of their intentions, a few hundred soldiers march along behind them.

Meniteith says to the others, "The English army is near us. Malcolm leads them with his uncle Siward and the good Macduff. Revenge burns in their minds, stripping out all other desires. But let's be honest. Their wounds are so grim that dead men would rise up to fight."

Angus says, "We will meet with them near Birnam Wood if we hurry."

Caithness asks, "Do we know if Donalbain will be with his brother?"

Lennox answers, "He is definitely not with the army, sir. I have the list of all of the peerage with them. Siward's son is there. And of course there are many young boys who will find their manhood in the battle."

Menteith asks, "And what is Macbeth doing?"

"He is fortifying his castle at Dunsinane," Caithness answers. "Some are saying he is insane to stay there, but some who do not hate him so intensely say he is doing it out of valiant anger. Either way, we can be certain that he has no control over himself anymore."

Angus says, "Macbeth must be feeling the blood of his murders sticking to his hands. Now, every minute he is hunted by rebellious armies for his treachery. I feel for those soldiers that follow him. They are merely following orders. They don't fight out of love for their king." Angus spits out a laugh. "He must know by now he is too small of a man to be a great king. It is like if a midget tried to wear a giant's robe."

"How can we blame him for acting so crazy," Menteith says, "when he condemns himself for what he has done?"

Caithness casts a reproachful glance at Menteith. "Well, let's just march on and give our loyalty to those who truly deserve it. We will meet with Malcolm, who is like medicine from the doctor to treat our sickly country. And we will pour every drop of blood in our bodies to help him rid us of this tyrant."

"Well," Lennox says, "maybe just enough as he needs to drown this weed known as Macbeth and water the royal flower so they may bloom. Whatever is needed, we will cast our lot with Malcolm in Birnam. I do hope some remains in our bodies though."

Chapter 3

"Don't bring me any more reports. Let all the thanes fly in the wind for all I care. I have nothing to fear until Birnam Woods pulls up its roots and marches on Dunsinane itself."

"Yes, sir," the doctor replies, uncertain of what Macbeth could possibly mean.

"What about Malcolm? Wasn't he born from a woman? The spirits that speak of the future told me that I shall fear nothing of a man that was born of a woman. So the disloyal thanes can fly and join with the weak English. My mind and heart will never wilt from doubt or shake with fear."

The doctor opens his mouth to speak but catches himself before saying anything. He looks over as a servant walks into the room. He takes this time to step back, hoping to remove himself from Macbeth's insane ramblings.

The servant himself is hurrying in his paces, pushing himself as fast as he can walk. His face is white as a sheet, his eyes open into round orbs.

Macbeth barks at the servant, "May the devil curse you, you white-faced fool! Why do you look like a frightened goose?"

"There are ten thousand," the servant begins, practically yelling in his fright.

"Geese, you idiot?" Macbeth chides.

The servant pauses with his mouth hung open in mid

sentence. "Soldiers, sir," he finally gets out.

"Go and pinch your face to bring color back to your cheeks, you cowardly boy. What soldiers do you speak of, fool? Curse you! Those pale cheeks of yours will frighten others as well." Macbeth stares at the man, who stands petrified by both the threat from without the castle walls and the raving lunatic before him. "What soldiers, milk-face?" Macbeth demands.

"The English force, sir."

"Take your face away from me."

The servant wheels around and practically runs from the loom, and Macbeth forgets about him almost immediately.

"Seyton! I am sick at heart when I see what this world offers anymore. Seyton, come here!" Macbeth stomps his foot while the doctor tries to remain hidden in the room. "This battle will either see me reign for as long as I live, or dethrone me. But I have lived long enough and have nothing to fear. My idiom is to wither and fall away, like a yellow leaf in autumn. All those things that come with old age will never be mine, such as honor, love, obedience, and many close friends. Instead, I have curses whispered against me in deep passion." He spits in disgust, as if trying to remove a foul taste from his mouth. "The honor of others goes no deeper than their voices. They say great things but act as cowards. My life lingers, but my poor heart would rather fail, but I cannot bring myself to end my own life."

He shouts out again, "Seyton!"

Macbeth's manservant enters, looking nonplused despite the king's ravings. "What is your pleasure, grace?" Seyton asks in his golden honey voice.

"What news do you have for me?" the king demands.

"I have confirmed everything that we have been reported, my lord."

Macbeth sneers, "I'll fight till the flesh is pulled from my bones. Bring me my armor."

"It is not needed yet, sir," Seyton says.

"I'll put it on anyway. Send out more cavalry to ride the country with orders to hang any who talk of fear. But first, bring me my armor." Macbeth begins to look around the room until his eyes fall on the doctor. "How is my wife fairing?"

The doctor steps forward to finally perform his duty. "She is not so much as sick as she is troubled with fantasies that keep her from rest. Nightmares, my lord."

"Then cure her of that. Can't you minister a treatment for a diseased mind? Pluck the memories of sorrow from her mind. Cut out the memories of bad times, and administer sweet oblivion through drugs. Pull out all the perilous stuff that weighs on her heart."

"I cannot, sir. The patient must treat herself to cure such ailments."

"Bah!" Macbeth spits. "Throw out medicine to the dogs. I'll have none of it." He suddenly yells, "Come and put on my armor. And bring my lance. Seyton, send the soldiers out."

Seyton begins to strap the armor onto the king.

The king's voice drops as he turns back to the doctor. "The thanes run from me doctor." He looks back to Seyton. "Come on and hurry!" Seyton pulls another strap tight on the chest plate, making Macbeth wince.

"Doctor, if you could, please see if you can find the disease that infects my land. Examine its urine if you must, but bring her back to sound and pristine health. I would praise you to the end of the world, where an echo will come back and praise you once more."

Seyton is pulling on Macbeth's boots now, trying to remove them to put on the armored ones. "Pull it off," the king yells.

"What drug would remove the English from our country? Have you heard of any we may try?"

"Yes, my lord," the doctor says. "Your preparations for war make us all hear something."

Macbeth begins to walk from the room, clanking with each step. "Seyton, bring my helmet and spear with you and follow me. I will not be afraid of death and destruction on this night. Birnam Forest will not march to Dunsinane." Macbeth leaves with Seyton close behind.

The doctor watches the march off and he says to himself, "If I were far from Dunsinane, I could not be paid enough to come back."

Chapter 4

"Cousins," Malcolm calls out the lords that stand near him on the edge of Birnam Woods. "I hope the day is soon upon us when people will feel safe in their own bedrooms once again."

Menteith says, "We don't doubt it!"

The English lord and hero Siward says, "What is the name of this woodland?"

Mentieth answers, "It's called Birnam Woods."

Malcolm says, "The woods helps hide our numbers, and it will continue to do so. Have every soldier cut down a branch and hold it in front of him. This way, we shall keep our numbers hidden, and Macbeth will not know how many march against him.

"As my lord commands," a runner answers before he bows and runs back to the camp to make sure the order is carried out.

"I just wish we have more news," Siward says. "All I know is that Macbeth sits overconfident in Dunsinane. Why would he remain there, allowing us to siege the castle?"

"It is his hope that we do," Malcolm says. "His soldiers are abandoning him whenever the opportunity is given regardless of promises of land or wealth. There are none with him except those who have been forced to. Not one fights because his heart is in it. This way, they are trapped, and a trapped animal fights most fiercely."

Macduff says, "Let's not make judgements now.

Assumptions have lost battles where the odds were even greater in favor of the win. Let's just remember we are soldiers, professional warriors. This is what we do. Let's do it well."

Siward says, "The time is approaching to begin the battle to find out if we have prepared enough or will be found wanting. It's too easy to think the battle is won before the first shot is fired, but the only way to know for sure is to proceed into battle and settle this debt in violence. Let's advance the war machine."

"Tell the troops we break camp!" Malcolm commands to great cheers from the others.

Chapter 5

"Even in waking now, I see the blood of Duncan. But why is it on my hands?" Lady Macbeth asks herself and she wanders through the courtyard, oblivious to the people running all around her as they prepare for the battle. The castle is dark as the sun is just rising, leaving the courtyard cast in shadow still.

"It was not my hands that did the deed. It must just be my guilt drenched mind." She rubs her hands together in a wet cloth, trying to get the blood off. "The spot just will not go away! Oh, curse Malcolm for fleeing on that day before he could be ridden of. I am sure it is him that marches on us, and it is that stress that so torments my mind. I must see my husband. He will do away with the charlatan."

She works her way through the crowd to the stairs that go up to the walls. She pushes her way past the soldiers who are marching to their positions on the ramparts. At the top of the stairs, she scans for her husband, looking to see where he stands giving commands. She finds him to the east and begins to make her way over to him but stops. Her hands rise to her mouth in shock.

The sun is rising up, casting a red glow over the horizon. Macbeth stands before the sun, making it look like a crimson corona glowing around him, fanning out as if the light comes from him. She laments how he looks bathed in blood. The scowl on his face, working with the shadows that dance across his features

113

reminds the lady of the devil.

"My goodly husband! What have I done to you? My Macbeth, you were a good man, a noble warrior. I pushed you to murder to take the crown for yourself. And this is the outcome? We are under siege both in castle and mind. We shall never know peace again, even in death. Our crimes do not allow for an afterlife without punishment."

She pulls a dagger out that was hidden in her cleavage. "This heart of mine is so heavy I can barely carry it anymore. Poor and kind Duncan, you will get your revenge." She raises the dagger above her head, blade pointed down. "I grant you avenged. May your peace come swiftly, husband."

Lady Macbeth plunges the dagger down hard before she can give her motivations any more thought. The blade bites deep into her chest, piercing her heart. Blood pours up over her hands, covering them with real blood for the world to see. She stumbles as the strength quickly leaves her limbs. Her vision narrows and black eats away at the edge of her sight, engulfing everything until she only can see a small spot before her. Her legs give out, and she feels herself falling through the ground. And then there is nothing.

****

"Hang our banners on the walls," Macbeth calls. "And keep the soldiers yelling 'They come!' And let them come. Our castle's strength will laugh at their siege. They will break, or they will sit and die of hunger and disease. If it were not for so many of our men revolting and joining these upstarts, we would have marched out to meet them in open combat, man to man, and driven them back to England. Treacherous curs."

A scream rises up from inside the castle walls, and others join in, all women.

"What is that noise?" Macbeth demands.

Seyton, who stands next to his lord, replies, "It is the cry of women, my good lord. I will see what transpires." He hurries off, leaving Macbeth among his soldiers.

"I have almost forgotten the taste of fear. The time is long gone when a shriek in the dead of night would have sent a chill to my bone, and my hair would have risen to stand on end from a ghost story. But I have filled my life with real horrors. The horrible is so familiar to my vicious thoughts that they cannot startle me anymore."

Macbeth feels a presence come up behind him unannounced. "Is that you, Beelzebub, come to collect my soul?" He looks over his shoulder. "Ah, Seyton. What was that cry?"

"The queen, my lord, is dead."

Macbeth looks forward again, down to the field below the castle, which will soon be covered in blood and the dead. "She would have died soon anyway."

Macbeth sets his face in stone, resolved to see through this task that unfolds. His wife dead. Everything he did was for her, for her happiness, and now she is gone. And all he has left is the mess of his life's misdeeds. There is only one thing left. "That was bound to happen someday. Tomorrow, and tomorrow, and tomorrow. Time creeps forward from day to day to the very end of recorded time, and every day past just brought fools that much closer to their deaths."

A runner comes up to the king and stands waiting to give his report. Macbeth ignores him. "Out, out, like a brief candle that burns brightly and fast! Life is nothing more than an illusion, a poor actor that struts and worries for his hour upon the stage and is gone henceforth. It is a tale told by an idiot, full of noise and emotion, but meaning nothing in the end."

Macbeth looks to the runner now. "If you've come to give me a message, they tell your story quickly. I have little time left."

The runner bows low. "My gracious lord, I am here to tell you what I saw, but I'm not sure how to say it."

"Just tell me what you saw and dispense with your idiocy.'

"Yes, my lord. I was standing upon the hill, watching for enemy movements over by Birnam Hill as you requested, and I know this is hard to believe, but I swear I saw the forest begin to move."

"Liar!" Macbeth shouts, his voice breaking. "Slave!"

"I would endure your wrath if I lie. You can see it for yourself though. Three miles from here is a moving forest, coming this way."

"If what you say is a lie, I will hand you from the nearest tree until you die of famine. If you speak the truth, you can do the same to me."

"My lord?"

"Dismissed."

The runner bows, fright showing in his eyes, and he hurries away, leaving Macbeth and Seyton.

"My resolution is beginning to fade. I now doubt what the devil told me though it sounded like the truth. What was it that I was told? Do not fear until Birnam Wood comes to Dunsinane. And now the wood marches on us. Arm! Prepare for battle!" he shouts. "If the messenger speaks the truth, there is no running away or staying here. I am growing weary of life. I wish to see the world plunged into chaos." He turns to the inside of the castle. "Ring the bell! Blow, wind! Come, ruin! At least we'll die with armor on our backs."

Chapter 6

The sun has raised high above the ground, allowing Malcolm to see the castle walls of Dunsinane grow larger as they approach. He cannot see soldiers upon the walls yet, but he knows the army is visible as they cross the fields leading to the castle.

"We are near enough now," Malcolm says to the solders following. "Lay down the branches and show who we are. Let fly our banners and beat upon our drums. Worthy uncle Siward, you and your son will lead the first charge on the castle. Macduff and I will do the rest, as our orders stand."

Siward says, "Good luck, future king. If we find the tyrant Macbeth tonight, then let us be beaten only if we cannot fight."

Macduff calls out, "Make our trumpets blast out. Loudly announce our coming as harbingers of blood and death."

"Advance!" Siward calls out to his troops. The host of soldiers split. The Scotsmen stay back, following Macduff and Malcolm. The English march forward, closing onto the castle. Malcolm leads his soldiers to the east and Macduff leads his to the west. Together, the three battle ready armies converge onto the castle of Dunsinane.

Malcolm hears the bells ringing from the castle, warning of the impending attack. As he charges forward, chanting reaches his ears, calling out "They come!"

"That we do," Malcolm says.

Siward's soldiers meet the castle walls first. Gunshots rain down upon then periodically, and they knock down a few soldiers from the walls with shots returned. Under the hail of lead rain, they push up on the iron gate that covers the main entrance, trying to force it open as others place thick logs to hold it up when it rises. The heavy gate does not budge though. The soldiers coming from behind bring tall ladders that they stick into the ground as they run forward, pushing the other end up to the castle walls.

Many of the ladders are immediately knocked back down, but so few defend the walls above. When only a few men climb the ladders, they already are too heavy to topple over. The men on the walls stand ready, waiting for the attackers to breach the walls so they can fight back. A couple try hacking at the top of the wooden ladders, but they have little success. Only one other ladder is pushed down, and those that have fallen are put back into place quickly. Siward's soldiers quickly begin pouring onto the walls.

With a beachhead established, they push on to the gate houses and turn the wheels, lifting up the iron gates. With the passages open, Siward's men rush in to face the lines of Macbeth's troops. Many of the soldiers standing before them are mercenaries, and among them there are many who throw down their weapons against the show of force they face, surrendering.

Siward's son leads the soldiers into the maw of the castle, fighting their way into the courtyard itself. As he enters the castle grounds, Macduff and Malcolm's men reach the other gates. They find similar weak resistance as they press forward into the open passages.

Chapter 7

Macbeth watches as his soldiers throw down their weapons, surrendering in an exodus from his command. Few stand to fight, and those who do are cut down quickly.

"They have me tied to a stake," Macbeth curses. "I cannot flee, but I will stand and fight like a bear." He whips around, looking for his doom. "Where is the man that was not born of a woman? He's the only man I am afraid of for nobody else can harm me."

"What is your name?" a young voice calls out. Macbeth looks for the speaker and finds him coming out of the mass of soldiers. He is a young man with handsome features. His sword drips with blood of his slain enemies, and his armor shows scratches and dents. He has fought this day, taking down some of the few men loyal to Macbeth.

"You would be afraid to hear me speak it," Macbeth calls.

"No, I will not feel fear even if you are one of the worst demons of hell."

"My name's Macbeth."

The young man does stop his pace for a brief second before continuing onward. "I am Siward's son. The devil himself could not say a name I would hate more than yours."

Macbeth raises his own sword now. "No, nor could the devil's name be more frightful."

"Frightful!" Young Siward spits the word as if it were

distasteful. "You lie, disgusting tyrant. With my sword, I'll prove your words false. Nothing is frightful about you anymore."

The boy steps forward while whipping his sword at Macbeth. The older man flicks his wrist and knocks the other's blade aside. He steps into the young man's guard and kicks at his foot. As his body leaps back, Macbeth stabs with his blade into the other's shoulder where the armor joint is weak. The blade pierces, though not deeply, it is the swords arm of young Siward.

"Not even a little frightful now, boy?"

Young Siward's mouth hangs open as he gasps for air. "You are a devil," he breaths hard.

"Maybe just."

Macbeth steps to attack again. The boy tries to defend himself, but his wounded shoulder does not allow him to raise his blade to block the attack. A small cut splits the flesh open on the boy's chin, making Macbeth smile in glee.

"It's the little joys in life that I have left to me," he says.

"Coward!" Young Siward yells and he switches the blade to his good hand and attacks.

Macbeth deftly hits the blade aside, comes back and slices the other's hand, making the sword drop from limp fingers. He stabs again, this time into a knee, making the boy fall earthward. Macbeth stands over him and swipes his sword once more, cutting the young man's throat with none of the ceremony of an execution. The blood pours out swiftly, and young Siward's limbs thrash about, refusing to let death take him easily but unable to do anything to stay the cold fingers. His limbs slow their movements as the blood stops flowing so quickly and ceases altogether when the spilt blood is nothing more than a trickle.

Macbeth looks upon the young man's corpse lying in the dust. "You were born of a woman. I smile at swords and laugh at any weapon brought against me that is held by a man born of a woman." He looks back into the fighting "I must find the one man who can kill me. Either he will bring me peace, or I will live forever." Macbeth leaves the courtyard, heading through a doorway and disappearing into the dimness of the castle's interior.

120

Macduff comes through the gateway as his men break through the lines of Macbeth's men.

Standing amid the chaos, seemingly unfazed by it, he shouts, "Tyrant, show your face!" He stomps to the middle of the courtyard. "Tyrant!" he again shouts. He turns slowly in a circle, muttering to himself. "If you have been killed by a hand other than mine, my wife and children's ghosts will haunt me forever. I cannot fight with these wretched men whose sword arms are for hire. Either I find you, Macbeth, or I will sheath my sword unused."

He looks back at the castle. "You must be there. Let me find you! Fortune, I beg for nothing more." Macduff enters the castle, following behind Macbeth.

The remaining soldiers that follow Macbeth fall asunder as more forces from Scotland and England fight their way into the castle grounds. Siward leads more of his men, as does Malcolm. The English lord shouts to the other, "This way, my lord. The castle's been almost captured with hardly a fight. Macbeth's soldiers are fighting against us, but many have turned to our side. Our thanes are fighting bravely. The victory is almost yours, and it seems there is little left to do."

Malcolm calls back, "We have met our enemies, and it is as if they try to not strike us."

"Leave the remainder of the battle for the others, my lord. Enter the castle, and let's have this ended."

Chapter 8

Macbeth runs through the halls of his besiege castle, trying to find the one man who can challenge him. "Why should I be a fool like the Romans of old and die by my own sword? As long as there are enemies of mine, I would rather my sword take them apart than me."

"Macbeth!" a voice demands. "Turn around, you hellhound. Turn and face me!"

The king stops his running and looks for who calls him. Macduff stands at the far end of the hall, marching purposefully forward. "Of all the men I have faced, you are the only one I have avoided, good Macduff. But go away from my sight. My soul is already heavily burdened by the blood of your family. I need not add you to those numbers."

"I have no words for you. All that I can say will ring from my sword. You are a villain bloodier than words can express," Macduff growls.

The nobleman attacks with his sword, swiping at Macbeth across his body. The king's sword rises and he steps back, pushing the blade away. Macduff moves to close the gap, swinging again in a short slice aimed for the other's shoulder. Macbeth's sword whips up, pulling the attack into the air and over his head. The nobleman disengages his blade and brings it back around only to meet Macbeth's once more. Their strikes continue, faster than the eye can follow, each intersection of the blades sounding out in a satisfying clang.

Macbeth crosses his body with the blade, extending his arm and blade away from the other, leaving his right side open. Macduff does not let the defenseless position go unanswered. He comes back around on that side with his weapon. Macbeth turns his back to the nobleman, stepping backward, placing himself against the other with his sword arm off to the right, which he pulls back in front of his face to catch the attacking blade. The two swords make a cross in front of the king, but a dagger in Macbeth's left hand pierces Macduff's abdomen. The nobleman moves backward, pulling the blade out of his flesh.

Macbeth turns around to face the other, smiling as Macduff clutches his side with his free hand to stem the blood loss. In a rage, the Scottish thane whips his sword toward the king, but the other steps to the outside of the strike and hits back with his sword arm's elbow to the throat. Macduff turns away, slicing upward as he falls back. In a flourish, Macbeth's blade twirls down and catches the other weapon, stopping the assault.

Both stand still save the rise and fall of their heaving chests. Their swords' tips are slightly cut into the wooden floor and crossed a few inches up their lengths. Macbeth's and Macduff's eyes do not wander from one another. The thane's face is full of resentful fury, while the king's merely appears bored.

"You are wasting your time. You may as well try to stab the air with your sword than to try and make me bleed. Set your blade against someone who can be harmed by it. I live a charmed life that cannot be ended by a man born of a woman."

"Then despair of your charm, Macbeth. Listen to whatever evil spirit serves you, and hear its words tell you I was not born. I was cut from my mother's womb before she could give birth to me. I am your undoing."

"Now I understand," Macbeth says mainly to himself in realization. "Curse you for telling me this. I feel the fear I had lost once again. Bah, I don't believe those fiends that whisper prophecies to me anymore. They trick us with words with double meanings, giving us a promise to uplift our hopes while breaking them in the truth of the meaning." Macbeth starts to back away down the hall again. "I will not fight you," he declares.

Macduff stalks the king. "Then yield to me, coward. You will live just like a deformed animal, paraded around for crowds to see you, to witness the deformity of your soul. We'll put a picture of you upon a pole with the words under it, 'Here you may see the tyrant.'"

"I will not yield," Macbeth yells. "I will not kiss the ground under young Malcolm's feet and be taunted by the common folk of the land. Even though Birnam Wood came to Dunsinane, and you oppose me as a man not born of a woman, I will fight to my last breath. I will cast aside my shield and strike with my blade. Let's have at it, Macduff. And the first to cry 'Stop, enough!' be damned."

Macduff lets go of his injury and lunges forward. Macbeth moves to block the blow and again counter, but his movements are twitchy, and not at all smooth as before. Their blades meet, and Macbeth's sword is flung from his grip, flying through the hall to imbed in the wall. The sword waggles there, almost tauntingly. Macbeth looks at it in utter shock, having never been disarmed once in his life. He looks back to Macduff. It is not the thought that death may have finally found him that bothers Macbeth so, but that Macduff looks so satisfied.

Macbeth falls to his knees in front of the other man.

"You are a murderer and a coward. You ordered my family killed. You couldn't even do it with your own hand. Coward! I wonder if you even killed Duncan yourself. I wouldn't be surprised if your wife had to do it for you."

Macbeth opens his mouth to answer, but he never gets the chance.

****

A trumpet blast carries over the castle. It is the sound of retreat as Macbeth's remaining forces pull out and begin to flee. Another trumpet cries out victory, and Malcolm's soldiers shout in joy.

"I wish all of our friends that have lost their lives could be here to celebrate with us, uninjured," Malcolm says.

Siward replies, "Some must lose their lives in battle. But I can see by those left, that this great victory was won cheaply. It cost us little of what such endeavors should."

"I suppose so," Malcolm says. "Macduff is missing still, as is your noble son, Siward."

"Macduff is missing, my lord," Ross says, "but we have found young Siward. He has paid the price of the soldier. He lived only long enough to become a man. As soon as he proved his manhood in battle, he also fell as a man."

"Then he is dead?" Siward asks.

"Ay, my lord. He has been carried off of the field already. Please do not lift your sorrow in equal measure to his worth," Ross pleads. "If you do, your sorrow will never end."

Siward ignores the tear that trails down his cheek. "Were his wounds on his front side?"

"Yes. On his front," Ross confirms.

"Then he is God's soldier now! He was no coward and faced his enemy that did him in instead of running. Had I as many sons as hairs on my head, I could not wish them a more honorable death. And that is all there is."

Malcolm says, "He deserves more sorrow spent on him than that, so I will mourn for him."

"Nay," Siward says. "He is worth no more. He parted well and settled his scores. With that, he is in the presence of God now! May we all be so lucky some day." Siward's eyes trail from the prince, and he stands gaping.

Malcolm and Ross look to where Siward stares.

"Hail, king!" Macduff shouts as he walks over to them from inside the castle. From his hand dangles the head of Macbeth, free of its body and held by the hair. His free hand clenches a wound on his side. "I call hail to our king because that is what you now are, Malcolm. Behold!" He holds up Macbeth's head for all to see clearly. "It's the tyrant's head. We are free from him. You, dear

Malcolm, are surrounded by the noblemen of Scotland, and they all think the same that I do. All of you, join me in cheer. Hail, King of Scotland!"

They all shout out, "Hail, King of Scotland!"

"It will not be long before I reward each of you as he deserves," Malcolm says to the men around him. "My thanes and kinsmen, you shall all henceforth be Earls, the first ever in Scotland to be honored as such. This is a new era for Scotland. We must now call all of our exiled friends back home, telling them Macbeth's tyranny is done. We must also bring to justice all of the ministers of the dead butcher and his demon-like queen."

Malcolm looks each one in the eyes for a few seconds apiece before continuing. "I thank you all, and extend an invitation to join me to watch me be crowned King of Scotland at Scone."

End

Endospore Sample

Endospore is the debut novel from R. A. Wilson, and one of the works he is the most proud of. It tells the story of a young man named Alan. Over a decade has passed since the Cataclysm left the surface of Ildor sterile. Underground Midgard was once the shining jewel of enlightenment and technology, but is now the last bastion of humanity, but it too is crumbling upon itself.

Alan lives contentedly with his lot in life, knowing little of the troubles swarming in the city. But when he returns home to find his parents murdered, he quickly discovers there is much to be outraged and angered by. Alan must first pull himself together if he is to discover the secrets of Midgard and why his parents were executed. And his only clue is a little biomechanical dragon called Ratatoskr.

A nontraditional epic fantasy mixed with post-apocalyptic science fiction, this is not the first book of a long, unending series, but a standalone story that possesses everything necessary to enjoy the adventure. It does not contain many of the normal fantasy or science fiction tropes either, leaving this story unique in a field where each book on the surface appears to be the same as the ones before. Endospore is something special.

127

WELCOME TO ENDOSPORE

The lights dimmed for the evening, as Alan walked home. In bed, he closed his eyes for a second. When they opened again, the lights were on full for the morning. It had been a dreamless night, and his body felt heavy as a rock. He performed his morning ritual, cumulating in breakfast of bloodcorn oatmeal, and leaves home for what he thinks may be the last time. He does not look back to it, longing in nostalgia. Alan refused to just be dragged along any longer. He already had made his decision, and he would fight to make it happen and live with the consequences.

He entered the Bazaar as all roads in the Nucleus pass through there, and the crowds fill in around him. Shops passed, though Alan took no note of them. He noticed little of his surroundings at all until a scruffy older man caught his ears. The old man was stomping back and forth, waving his arms about and talking to himself.

"No, I can't do that." He shook his head. "What do you mean? But I just can't." His face carried an expression of great remorse, and his eyes rolled freely about, seeming to not focus on anything. The eyes were unfocused and glossy, but when he happened to look at Alan, he stumbled toward the young man in great desperation. He fell into Alan, catching hold of his clothing. "It's you," he whispered as if it were some great secret.

His breath made Alan reel back and try to pull free.

"You can hear the voice too, can't you? He talks to you too, right? Surely you can understand. You do hear him, don't you? Your father does."

Alan pushed him away in disgust, sending the other to the ground. He walked around the sprawled form and continued on with more hurry than before as the old man kept calling to him. Alan found it sad that someone could be so lost in their own mind.

The crowds began to thin as he made way until breaking away from the people and leaving society behind as he made his way toward the little used cytotunnel that led to Bifrost's hideout.

Running through the streets once more, Alan's breathing

came in time with his steps and his heart rate remained steady. The distance passed quickly. As he drew near the cytotunnel, he heard voices. Alan stopped running and listened. He recognized the voices, making a smile overtake his face as he stepped in their path.

"Alan!" Tracy exclaimed. She ran over and embraced him. "I knew you would come back."

"I wasn't so sure," he replied. "I guess in the end there was no other choice though, was there?"

The man with her scowl. "What are you doing here?"

"I decided to come back. I'm taking George's offer."

"And he's coming with us," Tracy announced.

"I don't think so," he said. "There's a reason it's only us going on this mission."

Tracy said dismissively, "He'll be fine, Alex."

"Where're we going?" Alan asked.

"The Factory," she answered.

Alex complained more, but it was obvious Tracy had already won. Alex gave up complaining only when they walked up to the building they called the Factory.

It rested in the old industrial part of the Nucleus where most of the manufacturing capacity of the city was contained before the Cataclysm. With raw materials nearly inexistent as they used to be brought in from the surface, this area was abandoned. There were many buildings in this sector, but the Factory was unique in more than just its size. It was a whole complex, consisting of multiple buildings, all enclosed by a solid wall with only two gateways to allow people entrance. The gateway was barely standing between the walls, held up by one tired, old hinge, making the whole thing sit askew, allowing them to walk past unhindered.

They covered the grounds quickly and approach the largest of the buildings. It looked more like a warehouse than a factory to Alan. There was a large hanger door on its front, and it was held in place by a set of rails on either side. A smaller door was situated next to the hanger door, and it too was closed. The whole building was made of sheet metal, a fact that surprised Alan. If metal was so rare that Fredrick had hordes of people sifting through rubble to find discarded food cans, why would this building be left to rust?

And rust it did. Flakey oxidized metal, red in the dim, covered a good third of the building. The rust was so bad in some places that it had eaten small holes through the sheet metal. Through these holes, Alan could see how dark the interior was as no pinpricks of light shined outward.

Alex pulled on the smaller door, but it did not give. "It's locked."

"I still have a key," Tracy said. She stood before the door, and pulled a silver key from her pocket and unlocked the door with little difficulty despite years of disuse. She did have to shove hard at the door for it was rusted to the frame and swung on rusted hinges. She did not have the strength to open it. Alex threw his shoulder into it, but it remained solid like a wall. Alan also put his bulk to work, and the three of them got it to budge, though only slightly. The opening was barely large enough to allow Alan to squeeze through.

Even though light did not escape from inside the Factory, there was nevertheless a slight glow, but his eyes did not adjust quickly as it was nevertheless still very dim. Alan smelt rust and iron in the air, drowning out all other smells but a slight hint of grease. There were sounds as well, but they were so slight that Alan was not certain if he would have heard them in the light with his other senses not straining. It was a gentile scrapping, the whining of small electric motors, and the hissing of hydraulics. The odd thing was, the sounds were ever so slight but seem to be multiplied many times over, leaving Alan to feel like he stood amid a calm sea of sound. And over all of that was the pounding of machines, staying in tune to a beat of their own.

Alan's eyes began to adjust to the darkness, and the first thing he noticed was shiny red metal in small curved shapes over the floor, covering most of the large building from front to back. The curved metal moved, almost as subtle waves over the floor. And realization struck Alan as to what he witnessed, and he choked in fear. The floor was swarming with them, a seemingly unending supply of tormenters. He heard Tracy gasp as she too realized what they saw.

The floor was covered with hundreds of Copper Dragons.

Feeling trapped, Alan watched the dragonflies as they moved, expecting them to attack and overwhelm the three of them. Alan knew one alone would be enough to wipe them out, let alone the hundreds. Seconds tick by, and as nothing happened, a realization slowly crept over Alan. They did not seem to notice Alan and the other two. They moved about the floor randomly.

When he could finally speak, Alan asked, "What is this?"

Alex said, "This is the Factory, where the Dragons of Midgard were born. I don't know why there are so many dragonflies though."

Tracy said, "The system was set up for automated mass production, but it never was started."

"That's right. The final programming was not put in," Alex added.

"That would explain their behavior then," Tracy replied. "They only have the basic reflexes and no high functions."

"So they're harmless?" Alan asked.

"No," Tracy replied. "They act on reflex. They may lash out at anything that touches them. Maybe. Some of them might, anyway."

"What exactly are we doing here?" Alan said.

"We need the codes for the dragons," Alex answered.

"And where do we find them?"

"On the main terminal."

"Which is where?" Alan asked.

Alex said, "At the back of the building, where the dragons are manufactured."

Seconds pass in silence.

"So we need to go through them?"

Tracy said, "Yep."

Seconds more ticked by as the three just watched the biomechs.

"I'm game. How do we do it?" Alan asked.

"I have no idea," Alex said.

Alan looked at the programmer in surprise. "Then I hope the codes aren't too important."

"Extremely important," Tracy said.

"Maybe we can just try to walk through them?" Alan suggested.

"Be my guest, Alan," Alex said. "After you."

Alan looked back over the field of red dragons. He saw numerous ones snapping their neighbors when they touched. The teeth put gouges and scratches on the otherwise shiny red metal hides, leaving Alan to wonder what such a bite would do to his fleshy leg. The dragonflies all looked the same, gyrating in random movements, striking almost at random as well. As he scanned through their numbers, feeling numb, faced with such a conundrum, one Copper Dragon he saw was staring at him with a steady gaze, sitting, and not moving. The eyes did not waver, and Alan almost could not hold the stare.

Welcome, Alan. Ratatoskr's voice spoke in Alan's head. *Follow.*

Alan started to shake his head no, but he felt something rub against his pant leg. Copper Dragons had massed around him while Alex and Tracy had backed off as they watched them draw nearer. They stared at him in horror.

"I wasn't serious, you idiot!" Alex yelled, but while his mouth moved, Alan could not hear what he said.

He could not hear anything other than Ratatoskr.

Come.

Alan began to walk. The Copper Dragons swarming about his feet moved to let his foot rise and part to let it fall. Alan's eyes locked on Ratatoskr, the lone stability in the sea of chaos, and he followed it into the depths.

These creatures, my kindred, are sorry beings, for they don't even have souls.

"I didn't think machines have souls."

I might be part machine, but I am part biological as well. I think, I act, and I react. What is a soul anyway, but an insubstantial presence that feels it must inflict its will on the Universe.

132

"If that is the case, then it's the same with my people," Alan said to Ratatoskr. "They are merely sacks of flesh and blood with no desire to do anything but live. There is nothing left to mankind."

But that is merely because they have cast away their will to create, instead drowning in an endless cycle of consumption. My brothers here do not even have minds. They serve no purpose and must be turned off. Even in this state, their potential of disturbance is great, such is our power.

"You want me to shut them down?"

I will show you how. Just follow me and you will be safe.

"I will, if you help me find what I came here to get."

The codes for the other dragons? We have a deal then.

Alan was halfway through the factory when he stopped walking. Ratatoskr stopped as well and turned to him in almost the same instant.

Alan asked it, "Why do you keep coming to me?"

Ratatoskr said nothing, instead staring at Alan, making him uncomfortable. The dragonflies pressed in around his feet, snapping at empty air toward his legs.

"I just want to know. I'm nothing special, so why are you interested in me?"

Ratatoskr seemed to chuckle. *You seem to think this was all planned. Does it not occur to you that this is all merely coincidence? With enough coincidence, something can seem special, and then people start to think it is special, and that is all it takes. There is nothing special about you, Alan, but they are starting to think there is, and so you are special. It is the power of will, an intrinsic force, and this is just your perception of it.*

"So, I'm not really different then?"

You are the same decaying organic matter as everyone else. If anything, there is chaos in you, and chaos makes anything possible. For instance, look up, Alan.

Alan glanced to the ceiling of the Factory. He shouted in fright and nearly fell to the floor, keeping his footing merely by remembering what crawled around his legs. Suspended above his head were monstrosities, more Dragons of Midgard. Some were complete, but no life flowed through them. Others were merely parts of dragons, all suspended from the ceiling like macabre chandeliers.

So much of what we do comes from our power of will, and the more chaos one controls, the greater this power becomes, and the more dangerous. Physics calls this entropy, and the Universe moves toward the chaos because it is a more natural form of existence. The more chaos one has, the closer to the heart of existence one becomes.

"So the greater the chaos, the greater the potential?"

Close enough. The problem is, chaos is not compatible with orderly systems, such as life. It grows and takes all it can have, breaking down the order, killing it in many cases. All living entities are beings of order, but some like you have the chaos in proper balance with the order, unlocking great potential while preserving your order. Too little or too much chaos, and the whole thing falls apart. That is what was wrong with these failed dragons. They did not possess enough of the universal chaos to survive, or some had too much. But it is in you, Alan. So, are you special? No, you are not, but you have the potential to be more than most people will ever become.

Alan started to move forward again, uncertain of what he just learned, if he actually learned anything at all. He reached the far side of the Factory, where the great machine was building the homunculi dragons, the soulless dolls. Ratatoskr climbed on a computer panel and beckoned Alan to it. The Dragonfly instructed him how to shut the machine down, and he brought it to rest. A few more keystrokes after that, and all of the Copper dragons stopped moving and slumped to the floor, all but Ratatoskr.

"So, where are the codes for the other dragons?"

About the Author

I write things. More specifically, I write awesome things for awesome people. It was a long journey to publishing that first novel, mostly involving playing at made-up things with made-up people. So my insanity is questionable at best.

A lover of fantasy ever since reading the Sword of Shannara by Terry Brooks, I had no hope of escaping this fate. I have been accused of writing the worlds of Ravin Saga and a number of unrelated books, such as the children adventures of Little Kitten Mitten and the chronicles of when I went insane: The Wal-Mart Book of Ethics Abridged Edition.

I live with my cell mate and wife Alysia, as well as our son Atticus, in Gayville South Dakota. And yes, that really is the city's name, so just deal with it. We have four fuzzy, four legged children (Duke the Husky, Lucky the Chihuahua, Lizzy the Russian Blue, and Kirby the fat tomcat). Oh, and there is a turtle as well, but I don't really claim it. When not working at my day job or AlyMur Productions™, I spend every moment I can spare writing my next novel.

Source of original Shakespeare text and annotations

Crowther, John, ed. "No Fear Macbeth." SparkNotes.com. SparkNotes LLC. 2005. Web. 8 Jun. 2012.

www.ingramcontent.com/pod-product-compliance
Lightning Source LLC
Chambersburg PA
CBHW060618130626
46555CB00002B/561